STORM CATCHERS

TIM BOWLER

T0355143

OXFORD
UNIVERSITY PRESS

OXFORD
UNIVERSITY PRESS

Great Clarendon Street, Oxford, OX2 6DP, United Kingdom

Oxford University Press is a department of the University of Oxford.
It furthers the University's objective of excellence in research,
scholarship, and education by publishing worldwide. Oxford is a
registered trade mark of Oxford University Press in the UK and in
certain other countries

British Library Cataloguing in Publication Data

Data available

ISBN 978-1-38-200967-6

5 7 9 10 8 6 4

Printed in Great Britain by CPI Group (UK) Ltd., Croydon CR0 4YY

For Graham, Alison, Madeleine, and Jonathan
With love

'Evil for evil is justice
And justice is holy'

Aeschylus: *The Oresteia*

1

The sound came again, cutting through the night: a sharp, metallic tap that carried even to the first floor of the house where Sam lay sleeping. Ella stood over him and listened for it again but all she heard was rain spattering against the window. There was a storm coming—a fine start to the summer holidays—but that wasn't the problem.

The problem was being alone in the house at ten o'clock at night looking after Sam. She wished now that Fin hadn't slipped out to see Billy but it was her own fault: she'd insisted he go, telling him Mum and Dad would never know as long as he was back before they returned from the pub.

But that could be ages. Billy's parents had gone with them, which meant Mum and Mrs Meade would be yakking non-stop and Mr Meade would be trying to talk Dad into buying a new car from his showroom or joining the Save-the-Lighthouse project. They wouldn't leave the pub before eleven and Fin would take his time, especially as she'd promised him she was all right.

But she wasn't all right. She was terrified.

The sound came again, downstairs. She crept to the door. At least she hadn't undressed for bed. She'd been thinking of it but she was still in the jeans, T-shirt, and trainers she'd slopped around in all day, and now she was glad of it. It made her feel less vulnerable—though only a little.

She glanced at Sam. He looked so peaceful as he slept. She didn't remember sleeping like that when she was three and now, at thirteen, she hardly slept at all. She was scared of the dark, scared of the noises she heard in this ancient house, and now, after Mr Fenner's lecture in assembly about the need to be vigilant with strangers, she was even scared someone was stalking her round the village, though she knew that must be ridiculous.

Tap! The sound came again. She knew she ought to go down and investigate. Fin would. He might be small for fifteen but he'd go straight down and look the thing in the face. She made herself walk to the head of the stairs. Below her, the hall stretched away in eerie stillness. The lights were on but the house felt oppressive.

There's nothing wrong, she told herself, and started to walk down the stairs. It's just a storm coming. But it was no use. Polvellan was a house that had always frightened her even though she'd lived here all her life. It wasn't just that it was such an old building. There was something else, something she didn't understand; she felt uneasy here even when the others were around.

Tap! The sound snapped in the night again. She opened her mouth to call out and ask if anyone were there, then closed it again. If somebody were in the house, the last thing she should do was give herself away. She thought of Sam and wondered whether to go back and guard him.

No, check the downstairs rooms first. Make yourself do it. Then go back to Sam.

She tiptoed to the foot of the stairs and looked about her. On the wall nearby was the photograph of Dad at the opening of his Newquay superstore. Next to it were the sketches he had made of the Pengrig lighthouse ten years ago before the cliff-falls made it an endangered building. She ran her eye nervously over them, then scanned the hall as far as the front door.

Tap! She gave a start and looked to the left. The noise had come from the sitting room. There was no doubt about it. She stared at the door; it was ajar and the lights inside the room were switched off. She reached for the telephone. Ring Billy. Get him to send Fin home.

But she drew her hand back. She had to master this. She had to check the noise out for herself. It was bound to be something simple. She walked to the sitting room door and gave it a push. It brushed over the carpet a few inches and stopped. She stared through the gap, then took a deep breath, pushed the door a little further, and craned her head round.

The old room looked dusky but reassuringly familiar. Behind the drawn curtains she could hear the rain lashing against the window; but at least there was no one here. She pushed the door fully open and switched on the light. The features of the room sprang into focus: the piano, the fireplace, the armchairs, the sofa, the music stand with her flute beside it. She walked into the room.

Tap! She jumped. It was the window. Someone must be out there, hidden by the curtains. She hurried to the phone, picked it up and started to dial 999; then put it down. This was stupid. The tap wasn't regular. It might not be a person at all; it might be something trivial. What would Dad say if she called the police out for nothing? She strode to the window, pulled back the curtain, and burst out laughing.

It was nothing after all. A chain from one of the hanging baskets had broken loose and gusts were throwing it up at the window so that every so often the metal ring at the end struck the glass. Tap! There it was again. She chuckled and reached out to close the curtain; then froze in horror.

Reflected in the glass was a figure standing behind her in the doorway.

She whirled round. It was a man, a huge man built like a bear. He wore a black oilskin top and black waterproof trousers, all gleaming wet, and blue sailing shoes. The hood was up and fastened tight round the face, which was half-obscured by a scarf over the mouth and nose. She took a step back.

'Don't hurt me. Please don't hurt me.'

The eyes stared darkly at her.

'What do you want?' she said.

'You,' came the answer.

The voice sounded young but she had no time to think. He took a step towards her. She turned and dashed towards the bookcase. There was only one thing she could do but she had to do it now. He leapt after her but she reached the bookcase first, released the catch to the hidden door and slipped through. As she pulled the door after her, she saw his hands clutching for the gap.

She slammed the door shut and leaned against the wall, breathing hard. She couldn't stay here. He'd find the catch any moment and, besides, she had to reach Sam and get him out of the house. She hurried down the passage, feeling her way along the wall. It was too dark to see clearly but she knew her way from the old days when Fin used to dare her to go in. He loved having a house with a secret passageway; she hated it but it might help now.

She was halfway through already. It only went as far as the kitchen and she would have to brave the house again soon but it might buy time. She looked for the taper of light along the floor that marked the secret door in the kitchen wall.

There it was, just ahead. She felt round the panelling and found the catch. Behind her came a crash, a sound of stumbling. He'd found his way into the passage. She let herself into the kitchen and closed the door behind her. With any luck he wouldn't find his way out this end and have to go back to the sitting room. That might give her a few more seconds.

She ran through the hall as lightly as she could and up to Sam's room. He was still sleeping. She put a hand over his mouth and shook him. He stirred and looked up at her.

'Sam,' she whispered. 'Get up, quick!'

'Ella?'

'Sam, quick! We've got to get out of the house. And you're not to speak. Not a word. OK? Come on.'

She pulled at his arm but he resisted, still engrossed in sleep.

'Sam, please.'

Somehow she pulled him out of bed.

'Teddy,' he said, looking round.

'I've got him.' She grabbed Teddy from the bed. 'Come on. And not a word. Not a single word.'

She took him by the hand and led him towards the door, but it was no good. Already she could hear sounds at the foot of the stairs. She pulled Sam back to the bed and knelt down.

'Sam, listen,' she whispered. 'I want you to do something for me. Something that'll make me very proud of you. I want you to hide in your secret place and not come out till you hear Mummy or Daddy or Fin. Promise?'

'What for?'

'It's a game. A really important game. I know you can do it for me. Please, Sam. Please do it for me. Go and hide in your secret place.'

Something in her face must have persuaded him because he turned without another word, opened the wall cupboard and crawled in to the back, then pulled the big box of toys across so that it hid everything except his face. She passed Teddy through to him.

'Good boy,' she whispered. 'And if anyone opens the cupboard door, I want you to keep your head down so they can't see you. It'll be such a good game. When you hear Mummy or Daddy or Fin, then you can come out.'

'Ella?' His eyes were wide, unblinking. 'Are you going away?'

She leaned into the cupboard and kissed him. 'Just for a bit but I'll be back soon. Now be a good boy and don't make a sound.'

He said nothing but she felt his eyes on her face as she closed the cupboard. She stood up, stole over to the door and put her ear to it. No sound except the wind and the rain. She wondered whether she should try and hide somewhere herself.

No. If this monster searched the rooms for her, he might find Sam instead. She had to lead him away from the house. He wanted her anyway. She shuddered at the thought of what that might mean.

She heard footsteps creeping along the landing. They stopped. She slid to the side of the door so that she would be behind it if it opened. There was a long silence. The door opened a fraction. She sensed a huge form behind it; she sensed eyes peering, ears straining. She held herself rigid. The door opened wider and the figure entered the room. The face was still hidden by the hood and scarf. He took a step forward and stood by the bed, staring towards the cupboard.

She jumped out and pushed him hard in the back. He fell over the bed but quickly recovered and turned. She raced through to the landing and tore down the stairs. Behind her came the pounding of footsteps. She reached the hall and charged towards the front door in the white-heat of terror.

A hand seized her shoulder. She squirmed free and darted back down the hall. Again the footsteps thundered after her. She reached the kitchen, threw herself at the back door and wrenched it open. The hand caught her T-shirt and tugged her back. She wriggled free a second time and stumbled into the garden.

She was screaming now, screaming at the top of her voice. She plunged over the grass, struggling blindly towards the gate. If she could just get to the Meades' house . . .

But it was no good. He was already racing round the drive to cut her off. He reached the gate well ahead of her and turned to face her. She stopped in the middle of the lawn, the rain driving into her face, and saw him close upon her again.

Desperately she looked around her, searching the garden for sanctuary, but all she saw was tawny shapes moving like reeds in the darkness. She turned and fled towards the stable, knowing nowhere else to go. The building rose before her but she ran round as far as she could before the hedge stopped her. From inside the stable came the sound of Biscuit snorting.

The figure appeared at the side of the building. He wasn't running now. He didn't need to run. They both knew she couldn't escape. She stood there, her back to the hedge, her face, hair, clothes drenched. The figure moved towards her.

'What do you want with me?' she said. Her voice was snuffed away in the wind. She shrieked: 'What do you want with me?' He didn't answer and simply moved closer. She stared in dread, in disbelief. This couldn't be happening. This didn't happen to people like her. It happened to other people.

But it was happening. Now. She had to escape. He mustn't catch her, touch her, hurt her. She feinted to the right and raced to the left, straining to get past him. He caught her by the waist and picked her up like a doll.

'Leave me alone!' she screamed. 'Leave me—'

He dropped her to the ground, rolled her onto her front and thrust a knee in her back. She felt her hands whisked behind her and bound, a gag slipped over her mouth, then she was jerked to her feet and pulled, half-stumbling, up the slope.

She moaned and retched, struggling to escape, but it was no good. Her arm was locked in a grip so savage she felt it would crush her. She had to do something. Anything. She let her knees buckle and flopped to the ground.

'Get up!' he said. She didn't move. She couldn't move. She was too terrified to move. He pushed her face into the grass and she felt the knee in her back again, and this time his whole weight. 'Do that again,' he said, 'and I'll break your spine.'

He yanked her to her feet, tugged her to the front door of the house and pushed something through the letterbox; then he turned and pulled her towards the gate. She followed meekly. She was no longer resisting. She was simply crying. Crying as the rain drove into her face, crying as the gate opened before her.

Crying as he took her away.

2

Fin stopped outside the house, breathing hard after running up the hill from Billy's, and soaked through from the rain. He was later than he'd intended to be but the Meades hadn't come back so Mum and Dad should still be out. He stared at the gate.

That was strange. He'd made a point of closing it after him and no one in the house would leave it banging in the wind like this. Someone must have called. He hurried through, closed the gate after him, and ran up to the front door, digging in his pockets for the key.

Typical. He'd forgotten it—again. He'd have to ring. He reached out, then changed his mind. No point in waking Sam. With any luck Ella would still be up and in her room. He ran round the side of the house and stared up at her window. The light was on.

'El! Let me in!'

No answer. He heard a thud to the right. The back door was open, banging like the gate. He raced over and stopped on the threshold, peering in. The kitchen light was on and everything looked normal but he sensed something was wrong. He stepped cautiously in.

'El?'

All was silent in the old house. He hurried through to the hall. 'El? Sammy?' He was shouting now as fear overtook him. 'Where are you?' Silence. He reached the foot of the stairs and stopped. On the mat inside the front door was a slip of paper with writing on it. He picked it up and the words came at him like blades.

TELL A SOUL AND SHE'S DEAD.
WE'LL BE IN TOUCH.

'No!' he said. He leapt up the stairs and into Ella's bedroom. It was empty. He tried Sam's room. Empty. Mum and Dad's room. Empty. 'El? Sammy?' He charged back to the landing and raced through the house, checking all the rooms. They were not there. He slumped to the floor in the hall. What had he done? He'd gone out and left them and this had happened. He looked at the note again. *Tell a soul and she's dead.* No mention of Sam, yet there was no sign of him. He had a thought, thrust the note into his pocket, and bounded up the stairs to Sam's room.

'Sammy? You hiding?'

He didn't wait for an answer but simply pulled open the cupboard door and thrust the box of toys to the side. Sam was not there. He felt tears breaking out. This was all his fault. If he'd been here, he could have done something, and now . . .

He ran down to the hall and picked up the phone. He had to get in touch with Mum and Dad. They'd probably be having coffee with Mr and Mrs Meade. He dialled the number and waited. 'Hello?' said Billy's voice.

'It's me.'

'Fin?'

'Yeah. Are Mum and Dad there?'

'No, no one's back yet. There's only me and Angie here.'

'Oh.'

'Is everything OK?'

'Yeah, it's fine.' Fin remembered the note. He mustn't give anything away, especially to a chatterbox like Billy. 'I just wanted to . . . ' He thought for a moment. 'I just wanted to ask you and Angie not to let on I've been round this evening.'

'You asked me that earlier. I told you, it's no problem.'

'Oh, yeah. I forgot. Listen, I'll see you. OK?'

'OK.'

He put the phone down and checked his watch. Eleven o'clock. The pub would be closing but they might still be there. He found the number and dialled it.

'Coppa Dolla?' came the answer.

'Mr Langworthy?'

'Speaking. Who's that?'

'Fin Parnell.'

'Oh, Fin. Thought I recognized the voice. How are you?'

'Er, fine.'

'Stormy old night, eh?'

'Yeah. Are Mum and Dad there?'

'No, they just left with Stuart and Sarah Meade. Nothing wrong, I hope?'

'No.' He tried to calm himself. 'No, everything's fine. It was just . . . well, it wasn't anything important.'

He put the phone down, walked up to Ella's room and stood by the window. Below him the garden looked dark and forbidding. His eye fell on the stable. He ought to check that just in case. Biscuit was always jumpy when there were storms and if Ella had gone out to reassure him, Sam just might have gone, too. He ran downstairs and out of the back door into the garden. The rain had eased but the wind was still gusty and the night sky restless. He stopped outside the stable and called out.

'El? Sammy? You in there?'

No answer, save a whinnying sound. He entered the stable and Biscuit shuffled over.

'Have you seen them, boy?' He stroked the horse distractedly, his eyes searching everywhere, but there was no one here. Biscuit flicked his head back, then moved forward, nuzzling. 'Where are they, boy?' Fin held him close. 'Where are they? Please, where are they?' He felt despair closing upon him like a phantom—black, formless, terrifying— and he wanted to run, scream, strike out at it. He heard the sound of an engine in the lane and raced out. Mum and Dad's car was by the gate into the drive, the beam from the headlights thrown over the lawn. He gave a start.

Caught in the light just a few yards up the slope were marks in the soggy grass. He sprinted forward and knelt down. Beneath him was a confusion of footprints and further up a flattened area as though a body had rolled on the ground. He looked towards the lane and shouted. 'Mum! Dad!'

Dad was opening the gate for Mum to drive the car in but he turned at once. 'Fin? That you?'

'Yes!'

'Where are you?'

'By the stable!'

'You all right?' Dad came running over. 'What's up?'

'Ella,' he spluttered. 'She's been kidnapped. And Sam's gone missing, too.'

'What? What happened?'

'I don't know.'

'But you were here. You must have seen—'

'I wasn't here.' Fin looked down. 'I . . . I went down the road to Billy's.'

'You what?'

He didn't answer, didn't look up, couldn't look up.

'You bloody fool,' said Dad. 'You bloody fool.'

Mum arrived breathlessly. 'Peter, what's happened?'

'Ask Fin,' said Dad.

Fin felt Mum's arm round his shoulder. 'Darling, what's happened?'

'It's my fault,' he said, struggling to control himself. 'It's my fault.'

'Sssh! Easy now. Whatever it is, we'll sort it out together. Come on. We'll talk about it indoors.'

'But these marks—' He pulled away from her and pointed to the ground. 'You need to see them. They're clues. They're—'

'Later,' she said. 'We'll talk first. Come on.' She put her arm round him again. 'Inside.'

She steered him back to the house, sat him down at the kitchen table and pulled up a chair for herself. Dad stood over them, scowling.

'Now then,' said Mum. 'What's happened?'

'Ella's been kidnapped and Sam's gone missing.'

14

'What?' She jumped to her feet. 'Are you serious?'

He pulled out the note, tears swelling in his eyes again, and gave it to her. She read it at a glance.

'Oh, my God!' She thrust the note into Dad's hand and started pacing the floor. 'How did this happen?' She seized Fin by the arm. 'You must have seen something?'

'I didn't.' He was sobbing now. 'I didn't . . . see . . . anything.'

'He was at Billy's,' said Dad.

'What?' said Mum.

'It's true,' said Fin. He put his hands over his face. 'I went to Billy's. I know I shouldn't have. I got back and found the note on the mat. There was no one here. I . . . I looked in every room. I even checked Sammy's cupboard.' He swallowed hard. 'It's all my fault—'

'You're damn right it's your fault!' said Dad. 'What the hell did you go to Billy's for?'

'He's got a new computer. He wanted to show it to me. I was only going to stay a few minutes. El said she was OK on her own.'

'But she's not OK on her own! You know she hates being alone in the house.'

'I know, I know. I'm sorry.'

'How could you, Fin?' said Mum. 'How could you leave her?'

'She told me she was all right. She insisted.'

'That was just talk!' Mum shook him. 'You should have known that! You should have thought!' She let go of him and looked at Dad. 'We've got to call the police.'

'We can't. That could cost Ella her life. You've

15

read the note. If they see the police rolling up, they'll kill her. They've said they're going to get in touch. We've got to keep our heads till then.'

'But we can't just sit here!'

'Calm down, Susan.'

'Calm down?' She glared at him. 'Sam and Ella are missing and you tell me to calm down?'

'I'm just saying . . . ' He took a slow breath. 'I'm just saying we can't go to the police. Not yet anyway. It's too risky.'

'But we can't just do nothing.' She slumped into a chair, biting the ends of her fingers. Dad put a hand on her shoulder.

'The note only says *she* so Sam could be somewhere else. We can't call the police out but there's nothing to stop us looking for ourselves.'

Mum jumped up at once. 'Right, come on.'

'No,' he said. 'Not you.'

'But—'

'Wait.' He held her still. 'Someone's got to stay here in case the kidnappers ring.' She looked at him, her hands shaking. He stroked her arm. 'Try and calm down,' he said. 'We'll only make things worse if we lose our heads.'

'What do I say to them if they ring?'

'Find out what they want. Try and get to speak to Ella. Just . . . I don't know . . . just do what you think's right.' He fired a glance at Fin. 'You'd better come with me. See if you can do some good. And bring your torch.'

Fin wiped his eyes and stood up. Mum caught him by the hand.

'Fin?'

He looked away, unable to face her.

'Fin, give me a hug.'

He turned back and they held each other for a moment, then she kissed him on the cheek. 'Go on. Get out of here. Peter, leave your mobile on.'

'OK.' Dad nodded to Fin. 'Let's go.'

Fin sat in the car, numb with guilt, not trusting himself to speak. Dad backed them into the lane and they headed off down the hill, the squalls buffeting the car all the way.

'We'll check the village first,' he muttered. 'If we don't see anything, I'll have a look in the fields round the house and you can try the coastal path and the cliffs. Though I hope to God neither of them have gone that way.'

The Meades' house appeared on the right, the upstairs lights all on. Fin thought of Billy, no doubt still hunched over his computer, and turned away, unable to look. They raced as far as the village square and Dad pulled over.

'See anything?'

Fin stared through the gloom at the shop, the church, the school. There was no one to be seen. The lights were still on in The Coppa Dolla but there were no cars outside. He shook his head. Dad turned onto the Newquay road.

'We'll try this way for a bit. Keep your eyes peeled.'

They drove on, scanning the hedgerows as they flashed past, but there was no sign of anyone. Dad stopped at Ivor Brown's forge and backed into the entrance.

'No point going any further. We'll try the fields

and the coastal path. If they're not there, we'll take a look down in the cove.'

They drove back to the village square and headed for Polvellan. Fin forced himself to speak.

'Dad? Shall we go in and see if Mum's got any news?'

'She'd have rung.' The answer came curtly back. Fin looked away, fighting his emotions again. He knew this was all his fault. Mum and Dad were right. He should never have left Ella by herself. They all knew she was scared of the old house. He pictured her face as he'd last seen it. She'd seemed so confident and happy, so eager for him to go. He should have seen she was just trying to be brave; and now she was gone, and Sam was missing, too. If they were dead, he'd never forgive himself, and Mum and Dad would never forgive him either.

Dad drove past Polvellan to the end of the lane, pulled over and switched off the engine. Grassy fields stretched away on either side, wet and glistening in the sombre air. Fin stared at the forked track in front of them—left to the cove, right to the coastal path along the cliffs—and waited for instructions. Dad reached for the car torch.

'I'll try the fields. You check the coastal path. But listen—' His voice softened for the first time. 'Be careful. I don't want you going missing as well.'

'OK.'

'Meet back here in half an hour. I'll leave the passenger door unlocked.'

They climbed out of the car and switched on the torches. The wind was gustier than ever now that they were close to the cliffs, and the rain was starting again. Dad clambered over the gate into the field on

18

the left and vanished into the darkness. Fin set off towards the cliffs.

It felt spooky here. He'd never been this way at night before. He often came during the daytime, especially to wander down to the Pengrig headland and see the endangered lighthouse. It was only a ten-minute walk from home and there were never too many people around so it was a great place for thinking. He loved the view of the sea and, unlike more exposed parts of the coastline, the cut of the land offered enough protection for dense bracken to grow all the way down to the coastal path. The cliff-falls of the last few years had only added to the attraction of the place. But now, as he made his way through the storm towards the end of the track, he felt small and vulnerable and alone. He walked to the end of the rise and saw the land dip away.

There was the sea, bright with whitecaps; there were the cliffs; there was the coastal path; and there, running beside the bracken into the driving rain, was a small figure.

3

Ella stumbled into the cove and fell in the sand. The giant stared down at her for a moment, then tore back the hood and pulled off the scarf. She gasped. It was a boy—a boy about Fin's age by the look of him—but he had the strength of a man, the build of a man and, for all she knew, the desires of a man. She must not provoke him.

'Get up,' he said.

She tried to move. She didn't want to disobey him but the sight of this Goliath froze her into stillness. He hauled her to her feet and pulled her towards the rocks. She stumbled after him, tugged so fiercely she felt he would jerk her arm from her body. He pulled her into the shadow of the low rocks on the far side of the cove and drew her close. She stiffened as their bodies touched but his attention was not on her. It was on the cove, his eyes moving restlessly all around. She watched him warily.

He was searching for signs of pursuit. He'd been doing that even as they hurtled down the track to the cove, but he'd chosen his time and place well. Late at night and a deserted cove used only by the privileged few who had boats here. She looked over at *Free Spirit*, Dad's new motorboat tugging at her mooring close to Mr Meade's ketch, and wondered whether she was seeing them for the last time.

The boy started to pull her over the rocks towards the sea. She tried to call out to him but the gag prevented her and she could only moan. She knew what he was going to do now. He was going to drown her. There was nothing on this side of the cove but rocks and sea. She moaned again, beseeching him in the only way she could.

'Shut up!' he said, still pulling her along. She followed, unable to resist him, but with her hands bound and one arm held, she was losing her balance on the slippery rocks. He stopped suddenly, untied her, and ripped off the gag.

'Walk on.' He nodded towards the sea. 'That way.'

She stared at the rocks stretching round the side of the cove. A short distance ahead the coastline twisted to the right in the direction of the Pengrig headland.

'Hurry up,' he said.

She had to obey. There was no choice. Better to be drowned than beaten up and drowned. She could not escape this boy and she would never overcome him.

'Please don't kill me,' she said.

He simply nodded again towards the sea. She set off over the rocks.

So this was the length of her life now: a few yards, measured in faltering steps. She saw the water throwing itself against the land. It was growing rougher and rougher. The little cove was well protected but out here on its rocky horn, the sea rushed in unchallenged.

She wondered what he would do. Knock her out and throw her in or just hold her head under and let her slip away? She shuddered as these icy pictures filled her mind. The extremities of rock drew closer, bright with foam where the sea fizzed round them. The shoulder of land fell away to the right and she saw the dark form of the Pengrig headland and there, perched on top, the disused lighthouse poised over the sea, waiting for one last cliff-fall to send it to its death.

'Stop by the water's edge,' said the boy.

She stopped and turned away, unable to face him. This was the moment. She closed her eyes and braced herself. Loud in her ears came the hiss and crash of the sea; on her face she felt wind and rain and spindrift. She waited, trembling.

The blow never came. Instead she heard a voice. His voice.

'Move to the side.'

She opened her eyes and turned to see him pulling a dinghy over the rocks towards her.

'Move to the side,' he said again.

She moved, still trembling. The boy pulled the dinghy down to the water's edge. She glanced inland. It must have been hidden among the timbers of the old wreck just above the tide level. It wasn't a boat she recognized, just a tender that might belong to any of the cruisers round here. She saw two oars lashed to the thwart and a pair of rowlocks tied round them. The boy bent over to untie them.

She looked quickly around her. She had to make a run for it—now. She wouldn't get another chance. He straightened at once and looked at her.

'Don't even think of it.' A wave drove into the rocks and spray burst over them. 'Come here,' he said. She walked forward and stopped by the dinghy. 'Get in,' he snapped.

She stared at him. He must be mad. He'd never be able to launch the dinghy in water as rough as this. It would be dashed against the rocks.

'Get in,' he said, and she heard the danger in his voice. She climbed in and sat on the thwart. 'Not there,' he said. 'In the stern—the back.'

She knew where the stern was but said nothing and sat there. He put the rowlocks in place and positioned the oars.

'Hold the gunwale—the edge of the boat—on both sides.'

She gripped the gunwales tight. The wind was rising again but it was the sea that frightened her. He thrust the dinghy into a gap between two rocks, then, jumping in as he did so, pushed the boat off.

The sea threw them back at once but the boy was a match for it. Within seconds his oars were dipped and he was pulling the boat into the teeth of the waves. Ella clung to the gunwales as spray burst over the bow and splashed around the dinghy. The boy took no notice and strained at the oars. She watched, open-mouthed. It seemed inconceivable that anyone could have the strength to claw them away from the land, but the boy managed it.

For some time he toiled at the oars, then suddenly they were through the surf and the anger of the sea subsided, though the boat still bobbed in the swell. The boy rested for a moment, bent low over the oars, yet even like this he seemed to dominate the boat. She watched him uneasily, wondering where he would take her. There was nowhere round here that they needed a boat to get to apart from the three little rocky islands half a mile off the Pengrig headland and he surely wasn't taking her there. He straightened suddenly and started to row again.

Her mouth fell open. He wasn't taking her to the islands. He was taking her to Pengrig itself. She stared at the headland but the rain had closed in and all she saw was the darkness of the bluff and the vague outline of the lighthouse craning over the edge. A light winked off to the right. It was the new automatic lighthouse that had been installed when the old Pengrig light ceased operation. She stared through the gloom, wishing she could fly up to it, away from all this.

They drew in, the seas growing fiercer as the cliff loomed closer. The boy was breathing heavily now as he worked the dinghy towards the rocks. She gripped the gunwales more tightly than ever. What was he doing? Everyone knew how unstable the cliff was. There were notices on the coastal path, notices in the coves, notices on all the beaches, warning people not to walk close to the edge or take boats near the base of the cliff, and under no circumstances to . . .

She drew breath. Surely not. He couldn't be that stupid. No one would even think of doing such a thing. She watched in horror and saw that it was true.

He was taking her to the cave.

A plume of spray rose and splashed over them. She wiped her face and stared ahead. There at the base of the cliff was the entrance to the cave, bright with foam like rabid lips. She looked back at the boy, pulling them steadily towards it. He was taking them to their deaths. Even before the cliff started to collapse, the cave and the tunnel that led to the upper chamber were only visited in the calmest of weather. Now, with the coastline so unstable, no one went there; and only someone with a death-wish would try to enter at night and in conditions like these. She called out through the driving rain.

'Don't take me there!'

He took no notice.

'We'll die!' she yelled. 'We'll both die!'

He ignored her and continued to pull at the oars. She watched, shivering. The cliff was almost upon them. She saw waves breaking all around as eddies twisted the boat this way and that. Somehow the boy manoeuvred them through. The entrance to the cave yawned over them.

'Please!' she shouted. 'Please!'

He glanced her way, then pulled at one of the oars and spun the boat round. She leaned back with relief; he was going to take them away from here. Then she realized her mistake.

'No,' she said. 'Please no.'

But he was going in. He had merely turned the boat round to back them in stern first. She screamed at him.

'We'll die!'

He didn't answer. He was guiding the boat in, backwatering with the oars to keep them straight, but for the most part letting the waves surf them through the gap. She stared around her at the thundering seas. The boy seemed unconcerned as he brought them closer to the rocks. They were through the opening now and it was darker. The sound of the sea was louder, more frightening. She twisted round. There was the tunnel that led to the upper chamber where the smugglers used to leave their contraband, and there was the flat rock they used as a landing stage. The sea washed over it and crashed against the wall.

They could never land in this. The boat would be smashed to bits and they would be swept to their deaths. Even the boy, with all his skill and strength, would never get them in here. He turned to her.

'Get ready to jump out.'

'What?'

'You see that flat rock?'

She said nothing. He shouted.

'You see that flat rock?'

She nodded.

'You see the tunnel to the upper chamber?'

She nodded again.

'Can you see that jagged piece of rock just above the flat bit?'

She saw it and nodded. Spray burst over her face and she wiped it from her eyes.

'When I give you the word,' he said, 'you grab hold of that jagged rock, and pull yourself straight onto the flat surface and into the tunnel. You've got to do it all in one movement or you'll be washed away. Get ready.'

'But—'

'Get ready.'

She opened her mouth to beg but there was no time to speak. They were close in. The waves washed under them and ran up the wall, then, with a heaving roll, rushed back towards the sea. The boy guided them in closer, closer. The flat rock rose above her. She watched, waiting for the boy's command.

It didn't come. She looked round just as a wave struck, hurling the dinghy towards the rock; but the boy had been waiting for it and he steadied the boat as it rippled past.

'Now,' he said. 'Before it comes back.'

She pulled herself up onto the flat rock and scrambled across into the tunnel that led to the upper chamber. As she fell into the opening, she saw the wave surge back over the place where she had been. She wondered how the boy would land.

But he was not going to land. He was already plying his oars towards the open sea. She saw his form braced against the night sky as the dinghy drew level with the cliff-line. She screamed after him.

'Don't leave me here!'

She knew he would not answer. His attention was on the dangerous task of wrestling his boat away from the rocks. But he could see her. He was facing this way even as he pulled at the oars. She felt the tears start.

'Don't leave me here.' But she was murmuring now. 'Please don't leave me.'

The figure remained in view, pulling towards the sea, and it stayed there for what seemed a long time. He was taking the boat well clear of the rocks before turning away. She dropped to one knee, watching through the tears, and still the figure was there, that great bear of a figure, dwarfing that tiny boat.

And then it was gone.

4

'What happened, Sam?' said Mum.

They were in the sitting room: Mum drying Sam with a towel, Sam drying Teddy, Fin on the sofa with a mug of hot chocolate. Dad stood by the window with the curtains drawn back, staring out at the night.

Fin studied Sam's face. There was something strange about it. He didn't look like a boy who'd just had a terrible fright and on the coastal path he'd been running around as though he were playing with someone. He'd even been talking out loud, yet there'd been no one with him. Sam looked up at Mum.

'I'm sorry I ran away.'

'It's all right.' Mum put an arm round him. 'We're just glad you're back safely.'

'And Teddy.'

'And Teddy.' She reached out to help dry Teddy but Sam pulled him back.

'I'll do it myself.'

'All right, Sam.'

Fin caught Mum's eye and tried to force a smile. Sam always hated people doing things for him and his prim little reprimand had become a family catch-phrase. It was somehow reassuring to hear it now. But Mum didn't smile back. She seemed hardly to see him and her hand was trembling as she pulled Sam closer.

'Sam,' she said, 'you must tell us what happened.'

'I hid in the cupboard like Ella told me to.'

'Your secret cupboard? The one in your room?'

'Yes.' Sam dabbed the towel over Teddy's face. 'She told me to stay there and not come out till you came back.'

'Good boy,' said Mum. 'Now, why did she ask you to hide in there? Do you know?'

Sam shook his head.

'All right. What happened next?'

'I heard noises in the house.'

'What kind of noises? Shouting?'

'Running.' Sam looked round at them. 'Where's Ella? Is she in bed?'

Fin gave a start. Somehow it hadn't occurred to him that Sam didn't know she was missing. Dad answered. 'She's not here at the moment, Sam. She's gone away for a little while.'

'She promised she was coming back.'

'What did she say?'

'She said she was going away and I was to be a good boy and hide in the cupboard and she said she was going to come back. She promised.'

Fin knelt down and looked him in the face. 'Then she will be back, very soon.' He paused. 'Sammy, if Ella told you to stay in the cupboard till Mummy and Daddy got back, why did you leave it and run away to the cliffs?'

Sam's mouth quivered. 'It's a secret.'

Fin frowned. Sam always had lots of secrets, things he only confided to Teddy. He thought over the little boy's behaviour on the coastal path. It was certainly

29

strange but there was one possible explanation for why he'd left the cupboard.

'Sammy, was it one of your secret friends who told you to leave the cupboard and run to the cliffs?'

Sam hesitated, still clinging to his secret, then he nodded. Fin glanced at Mum and Dad. They looked tired and tense and frightened. Mum was struggling to stay calm and Dad seemed ready to snap. But at least some kind of picture was emerging. Ever since Sam had learnt to speak, he'd been talking about his 'friends'. They were part of his imaginary play-world and only he and Teddy could see them. It had always been harmless enough.

But he had never run away to the cliffs before.

Fin knew there was no point in questioning Sam further. He always grew upset if he felt people were doubting the existence of his make-believe companions; and besides, he was exhausted. Mum picked him up. 'Come on, Sam. Bed.' And she carried him from the room.

Fin stood up and joined Dad by the window and they stared out together in silence. From the other side of the pane the night seemed to scowl back at them. The rain had stopped but squalls from the sea still stirred the bushes into uneasy movement.

'Dad?' said Fin.

'What?'

'I found a window open in the drawing room.'

'So?'

'Well—maybe they got in that way.'

'Who gives a damn how they got in?' Dad grunted. 'They've got what they wanted, thanks to you. All we can do now is think about how to get her back.'

Fin turned away, guilt flooding over him once

more, and retreated into silence. Mum returned a few minutes later. She looked dazed and anxious.

'He's asleep,' she said. 'I was worried he might be too upset but he went out like a light.' She sat on the edge of the sofa, looking nervously up at them. 'I'm so frightened. Why haven't we heard from the kidnappers?'

'They'll ring,' said Dad.

'But it's ages since they took her.'

'We've got to keep calm. We mustn't go to pieces.'

'Dad?' said Fin.

'What?'

'Are you sure we can't go to the police?'

'It's too risky.'

'But you know people, lots of people. In the police, I mean.'

'What's that got to do with it?'

'Well, they'd . . . they'd be careful.'

'Fin's right,' said Mum. She looked eagerly at Dad. 'They'd be careful. They wouldn't do anything silly. They'd—'

'It's still too risky,' said Dad. He glared at her. 'For Christ's sake, I'm not putting Ella's life in danger until we know more about the kidnappers and what their demands are. If we panic now, we could blow everything and lose her. Is that what you want?'

'Of course not.'

'If we haven't heard from them by mid-morning, we'll think again about the police, but right now we've got to wait and hope they ring.'

'Well, why don't they?' said Mum. She stood up and started to walk up and down the room. 'This is driving me mad and now Sam running away, too. I don't understand it. I know he's got his games of make-believe but he's never done anything as crazy as run to the cliffs before.'

'He was probably out of his mind with fright,' said Dad. 'Think about it. Ella makes him hide in the cupboard, then he hears the pounding of feet and suddenly he's left on his own. The wind's getting up and the rain's beating on the windows. He probably starts calling for Ella and there's no answer. He could easily have panicked and run out to try and find her, or us, and maybe—just maybe—he blundered up to the cliffs.'

'But he said one of his little friends told him to leave the cupboard.'

'He probably just made that up. You know what a vivid imagination he's got.'

The phone rang and Dad lunged for it.

'Press the speaker button so we can hear,' said Mum.

Dad took a deep breath and pressed the button. 'Hello?'

'Mr Parnell. What a pleasure to speak to you. I've been looking forward to this conversation so much.' It was a boy's voice and sounded to Fin like someone about his own age. It was brash and confident and mocking, and he hated it at once.

'Who are you?' said Dad.

'You've got your telephone speaker on. I can hear. That means you're all listening.'

'Who are you?'

'Maybe Mrs Parnell's there, too.' There was a silence, as though the caller were waiting for some confirmation. None of them spoke and he went on.

'And maybe that little kid with the teddy bear. Or is he sleeping?'

'I said, who are you?'

'And maybe that other boy's there. The boy with the blue jacket. Are you there, boy with the blue jacket?'

Fin saw Dad's eyes swivel towards him and knew he was to remain silent, but he wanted to answer so much. He wanted to tell this boy what he thought of him, what he'd do to him if he hurt Ella. The voice went on.

'I hope you are because I'm really grateful to you. If you hadn't gone out this evening, I'd never have got her. Are you listening to this?'

'I'm listening, you bastard!' said Fin, unable to contain himself. Dad glared at him but Mum reached out and took his hand. There was a chuckle at the other end of the line.

'So you are there. That's nice.'

'What do you want?' said Dad.

'A hundred thousand pounds in cash by Wednesday,' said the voice calmly.

'I want to speak to Ella.'

'Not possible, I'm afraid.'

'How do I know she's not dead?'

'You don't.'

'So how can I trust you?'

'You can't.'

Fin let go of Mum's hand and clenched his own into a fist. The arrogance of the voice made him want to smash the phone.

'I have to have some proof she's alive,' said Dad.

'Well, you can't.'

'Then I can't give you anything.'

'So she dies. Bye.'

'Wait!' Dad clutched at the phone as though somehow he might catch hold of the person at the end of the line. There was a tense silence but no click. 'Wait,' he said. 'For God's sake, just . . . wait.'

Silence.

Dad went on, slowly. 'I don't seem to have much choice, but look, I don't know if I can fix this by Wednesday.'

'Of course you can.' The voice tutted. 'Do you think I don't know who you are? You're Mr Multimillionaire, Mr Success, Mr Pillar of the Community, Mr Magistrate. You own a chain of supermarkets all over Cornwall. You've got the biggest, poshest house in Trevally. You've got land. You've got a big new motorboat. Your daughter rides a thoroughbred. Your wife wears expensive clothes. You've got two flash cars. You can do anything you want. You say jump and people jump.' The voice lowered. 'Get the money by Wednesday if you want to see your daughter alive.'

Mum rushed over to the phone, unable to keep silent any longer.

'Listen, whoever you are, we'll find the money but you must promise you won't hurt her.'

'I'm making no promises. Get the money and we'll take it from there. I'll give you till Wednesday lunchtime.'

'But it's the small hours of Tuesday now,' said Dad.

'Then you've got no time to waste. And remember what I said in the note. You don't tell anyone about this. Not a soul. You don't tell your friends or your business contacts or your cosy little mates in the police force. If I find out you've been blabbing, you'll get your daughter back one piece at a time.'

There was a click and the voice was gone.

5

Ella sat by the opening to the tunnel, staring towards the mouth of the cave and the open sea beyond. She had not moved for some time. She was wet, shivering, and still crying. A few feet below her the sea surged in, rushed as far as the wall, then raced out again.

She followed it with her eyes, the way the boy had gone. It was still night, though the sky was no longer black. It was grey: deep, dark grey. There was no escape. The walls of the cave offered nothing for her to climb along and even if she made it to the entrance, she would still have a sheer cliff-face above her. She looked round at the tunnel that climbed to the upper chamber.

Only a few weeks ago Mr Cunningham had been rambling on in Geography about this place: how the cliffs had formed and the cave had been gouged out, and how pressure from the sea had forced air in and created the tunnel. It had all seemed so safe in the classroom. Now she was seeing it for herself. She had no desire to go up but she knew she couldn't stay down here for ever. One lapse of concentration, one freak wave, and she could be swept away like a leaf.

She stood up and stepped into the tunnel. Darkness enveloped her at once. She put her hands out and felt her way along the walls. They were cool and hard and bony, and they closed in quickly on either side. The ceiling was low and made her stoop but it was the floor that was dangerous. The rock had formed a rough, twisting stairway, which made climbing easier, but in the darkness she could not see the steps. If she fell, there would be no one to help her—assuming she was alone here.

She forced herself to climb on, testing the ground ahead with a foot before inching forward. At least she was moving away from the sea but she was frightened of what lay ahead in the darkness. How far the tunnel went she did not know and could not see.

She climbed for several minutes, the smash of the waves still loud in her ears, then suddenly the ground flattened out and she caught a hint of light ahead. She took a few more steps, her hands away from the walls now that she could see better, and saw a series of tiny gaps in the rock. She stopped by the first and put an eye to it.

It was moonlight that was coming through. There was the night sky and there below her the base of the cliff. She moved round to the next gap and squinted through. Now she could see the rocks by the entrance to the cave. There was a ring of froth around them. She must have climbed about fifty feet. She moved back from the gap and looked round, and realized that the tunnel had come to an end.

She had reached the upper chamber.

It was only a small space, hardly bigger than Mum and Dad's bedroom. To her relief, the ceiling was high enough for her to stand upright and with the wind whistling through the gaps the chamber was at least dry. No wonder the smugglers had left things here—but they were not the only ones to do so.

In the far corner she saw three large boxes and what looked like a bucket. She walked over, still shivering, and knelt down. The first box was full of bottles of mineral water; the next contained an old towel and a couple of thick blankets. She pulled one out and draped it around her shoulders. It smelt musty but she was grateful for the warmth. She opened the last box and saw packs of sandwiches inside. She held one up and tried to read the label.

Tears filled her eyes. It was from Parnell's Superstore. The Newquay branch. She stared at it. Cheese and chutney. Sell-by date: tomorrow. She picked up one of the bottles of mineral water and studied the label. It, too, was from the Newquay branch. She cradled the bottle in her arms and went on crying.

And as she cried, she pictured Viv and Sally and Karen and Steve at the checkouts, and Sophie at the information desk, and Patrick and Barnaby stacking the shelves and flirting with the customers, and Brian and Melanie, and all the others. She wiped her eyes and looked at the other sandwich packs in the box. Cheese and tomato, egg and cress, tomato salad. At the bottom of the box were bags of apples and bananas, all from the Newquay store.

She slumped to the ground, trying to think, but she could not. She could only feel; and what she felt was pain. She let her back rest against the rocky wall, wrapped the blanket tightly around her, and drew her knees in to her chest, and stared ahead, quivering, numb.

It was a long time before she stirred. She did not know where her mind had been; she only knew that she had not slept and that the storm was easing. She opened a pack of cheese and chutney sandwiches and started to eat one of them. It tasted good. She finished both sandwiches in the pack, opened another and quickly consumed two more. Her eyes fell on the bucket. She pulled it towards her and saw something behind it.

A pack of loo rolls, bought—like everything else—from Parnell's. Maybe it was some kind of taunt, or maybe just coincidence. Whatever the reason, the boy had obviously planned this thoroughly, otherwise he wouldn't have gone to the trouble of providing food and drink and blankets and this crude toilet arrangement. Maybe he wasn't going to kill her after all and just wanted money from Dad; in which case she might have a chance of getting out of this.

She closed her eyes and tried to sleep, but all she could think of was Sam's face peeping out of the cupboard at her, and Fin, dear old Fin. He would never forgive himself for leaving her alone.

Fin sat on the edge of his bed, staring at the wall. He had done as Mum had told him—gone to his room, tried to rest—but it was no good. He knew he wouldn't sleep, any more than Mum and Dad would; and they weren't even bothering to try. Even now he could hear them downstairs, pacing the sitting room floor.

He walked over to the window of his room and drew back the curtain. The darkness was easing and dawn was near, and the worst of the storm seemed to be past. His reflection stared back at him, blurred against the grey and tinged with the features of the garden pressing through. He found his mind playing tricks and for a moment imagined Ella's face before him in place of his own. He leaned his forehead against the glass and closed his eyes.

'El,' he murmured. 'I'm sorry.'

He heard a voice out on the landing, a small, trembling voice. He whirled round and stared through the half-open door of his room but there was no sign of anyone. He opened the door fully and peered out. Sam was standing at the top of the stairs, staring down towards the hall. The voice came again, and it was Sam's, yet it sounded strangely dream-like.

'I can't come. I promised Mummy.'

Fin tiptoed up behind him, watching in case Sam stepped closer to the stairs, but the little boy did not move. He seemed transfixed. Fin bent down, ready to catch him if he fell.

'Sammy?' he said softly.

Sam turned and Fin studied his face. The eyes were wide. They seemed to look through him as though he were a ghost.

'It's me, Sammy. It's only me.'

He heard the footsteps in the sitting room cease but kept his eyes on Sam. 'What's up, Sammy?'

'Is Ella going to die?'

'Of course not. She'll be back soon.'

Sam looked round at the stairs as though he'd heard something. Fin followed his gaze but saw nothing.

'Who are you talking to, Sammy?' Sam's lips tightened. Fin put his arms round him. 'It's all right. You don't need to tell me if it's a secret. You tired?'

'I want Ella to come back.'

'She will. Soon.' Fin saw the sitting room door

open a fraction and a moment later Mum's face peeped out. Their eyes met and he motioned that all was well. She nodded and closed the door quietly once more. Fin stroked Sam's head. 'She'll be back soon, Sammy. I promise.'

'Is she thinking about us?'

'Yes.'

'Right now?'

'Yes, Sammy.' He kissed Sam's head. 'She's thinking about us right now.'

6

The phone rang at half past eight in the morning. They were in the kitchen, slumped round the table with breakfast barely touched. Only Sam had been to bed. Dad jumped to his feet.

'I'll get it.'

'Take it in the sitting room,' said Mum. She glanced at Sam, who was drinking a glass of orange juice. 'And close the door behind you.'

Fin followed Dad out of the kitchen, closed the door behind them, and hurried with him to the sitting room. Dad pressed the speaker button on the phone. 'Hello?'

'Hi, Mr Parnell.'

Fin relaxed. It was only Billy.

'Hello, Billy,' said Dad. 'How are you?'

'Fine, thanks.'

'That was some storm we had last night.'

'Yeah.'

'Still, looks like we're in for a nice day today. Mum and Dad OK?'

'Not really. Well, Mum's OK. Dad's getting on everyone's nerves. He never knows what to do with himself when he's on holiday.'

'I'm not much better myself. Anyway, what can I do for you?'

'Is it still on for this afternoon?'

'This afternoon?'

'The trip in your new boat. You did promise. Only I expect you're busy. Dad said you're bound to call it off.'

'He said what?'

'He said you're always cancelling golf matches and things because you're too busy.'

Fin rolled his eyes at Billy's legendary lack of tact.

'The boat trip's still on,' said Dad.

'Great. Could I speak to Fin, please? And Angie wants a word with Ella afterwards if she's there.'

Dad paused. 'Ella's not here right now.'

'Oh, OK. Look, could you hold the line a moment?'

'Sure.'

Fin heard Billy shouting at the other end.

'Angie? She's not there.' He didn't hear Angie's reply but Billy was soon back. 'Angie says could Ella ring her when she gets in?'

'I'm afraid she won't be back for a few days.' Dad's eyes flickered at Fin. 'She's gone to London to stay with Auntie Jean and Uncle Frank. I'm sure she must have mentioned it to Angela.'

'Don't think so,' said Billy. 'I'll tell her anyway. Is Fin there?'

'Sure. I'll put him on.'

Dad picked up the phone, put his hand over the mouthpiece and switched off the speaker. 'Now listen, Fin, you heard what I just said and that's the line we're going to take. She's gone to stay with Auntie Jean and Uncle Frank. If you mess it up and give away what's happened, Ella could die.'

'I know that,' said Fin. 'But what did you have to agree to the boat trip for?'

'What choice did I have?' Dad scowled at him. 'I don't want to go any more than you do. I'd forgotten about the bloody thing with all this going on but we've got to act as though everything's normal. And if Billy wants to meet up with you, agree to it, even if you're not in the mood. Don't give him the impression anything's wrong. Only don't bring him here if you can help it. Try and meet up at his place.'

'All right.' Fin took the phone. 'Hello?' he said.

'Fin, hi. You coming over?'

'So what's up with you?' said Billy.

Fin looked at him. He'd been sitting on the bed in Billy's room for half an hour and had hardly said a word. Billy had been at his desk, chattering on in his usual fashion about computers and stones and star-gazing and the thousand and one other subjects he tended to flit between in the course of a normal conversation, and Fin had supposed his inwardness had not been noticed. But he was wrong.

'What's the problem?' said Billy.

Fin tried to think of something. Billy was a good friend in many ways but he was the last person in the world he could confide in. The news would be round the village by the end of the day and probably most of Newquay as well.

'I fell out with Mum and Dad,' he said eventually.

Billy gave him a grin. 'Know how you feel. I'm always falling out with my mum and dad. Usually about the state of this room.'

'Can't say I blame them,' said Fin, glancing round.

There were books everywhere, packed into the shelves or strewn over the desk, the bed, the floor. He had books on astronomy, astrology, ley lines, weird cults, hypnotism, crop circles, and Indian mystics. Interspersed with these were computer manuals, football magazines, books on the smuggling that used to go on round the coastline, and pamphlets about Mr Meade's campaign to save the Pengrig lighthouse. And that was just the reading material. Scattered round the room were pebbles, shells and bits of flotsam that Billy had collected from the beaches, and clothes that he had dropped to the floor and Mrs Meade had refused to pick up. Billy's was an enquiring mind but not an organized one. Angie appeared in the doorway.

'When's she coming back?' she said.

'Sorry?' said Fin, though he knew what she meant.

'When's Ella coming back from London?'

'I don't know.'

'She's not going to be away for the whole of the holidays, is she?'

'Oh, no. I'm sure she'll be back before the end.'

'But you must know how long she's going to be away.'

He tried to sound casual. 'It's a bit open-ended. Mum and Dad only fixed it at the last minute.'

'But why's she gone away anyway?'

'Auntie Jean and Uncle Frank haven't seen her for ages and she wanted a chance to go round London with them.'

'She could have told me. We were supposed to be going riding after the boat trip this afternoon.'

'Yeah, well, like I say, they only fixed it at the last minute.'

He wished she would go away—he could tell she didn't believe him—but she eventually shrugged and left. He looked at Billy, who was fiddling again with his new computer.

'Billy?'

But his friend was absorbed and had probably heard nothing of the conversation with Angie. Instead he was tapping keys and staring at the screen. 'I can't get my head round this software,' he said suddenly. He clicked the mouse and nodded towards the screen. 'See? It's not meant to do that. I'll have to get Dad to help me when he comes in.' He looked round. 'What did you want to ask me?'

'If you lost something, what would you do?'

'Lost something? Like what?'

'I don't know, a book or a pen, or maybe something a bit more valuable.'

'What, like a watch?'

'Yeah, or a wallet with lots of money in it. What would you do?'

'Don't know. Panic, I suppose.'

'No, I mean if you'd looked everywhere and still couldn't find it, and you'd asked everybody and nobody else could find it, what would you do then?'

Billy scratched his chin. 'Give up, I guess. Why? What have you lost?'

'It's not me. It's Sammy. He lost Teddy the other day. He was in a real state about it. You know, tears and stuff. But I just wondered . . . what we could have done.'

'Could have done? What, you mean you've found Teddy?'

'Oh, yeah. He turned up eventually.'

Fin gave an awkward smile. He knew this was a

46

strange line of conversation to be pursuing, especially as it was based on a lie, but the fabrication about Teddy was the only thing he could think of in a hurry. Billy stared at him.

'If you've found Teddy, what's the problem?'

'Oh, I was just wondering what we could have done. Don't worry. Forget it.'

'I mean, if something's lost, it's lost and if it's found, it's found. I don't get what you're asking me.'

'Yeah, it's stupid. Forget it.'

He felt an idiot now, but he'd been thinking of Ella and it just struck him Billy had so many crazy theories about things, he might have been able to suggest some course of action; and action was what Fin needed right now. This waiting was becoming unbearable.

Billy said nothing for a while and went on clicking the mouse and tapping keys, then suddenly he stopped and looked round again. 'I suppose you could have tried dowsing.'

'Say that again.'

'Dowsing. You know. When people want to find things, they sometimes dowse for it.'

'But that's . . . I mean . . . that's for water, isn't it?'

'No, anything you like. Hang on.'

Billy jumped up from the desk, stood on the bed next to where Fin was sitting, and ran his finger along the books on the top shelf. How he could make out what was there was beyond Fin. The shelf—like all the other shelves—was bursting with books, but they were in no order whatsoever. Some were horizontal, some vertical, some had spines facing inward, some outward, some were upside down; several were hidden completely because Billy had draped his wetsuit over them. But Billy clearly knew what he wanted and a moment later his hand darted out and pulled down a small book.

'There you go.' Billy threw it down. 'Cop a load of that.'

Fin caught it and read the title aloud.

'*The Magic Pendulum*.' He glanced up at Billy. 'What's this got to do with finding things?'

'God, you don't know anything, do you?' Billy jumped down and sat on the bed next to him. 'There's different kinds of dowsing. You can use one of those stick things, you know, or they've got . . . kind of . . . rods you hold on to. I've got a book about that, too, somewhere.' He glanced along the shelves again.

'Don't bother,' said Fin.

Billy looked back and took the book from him. 'Anyway, you can use a pendulum for dowsing as well. There's a chapter on it.' He flipped through the pages. 'There you are.'

Fin was rapidly losing interest but he glanced down. On the page before him was a chapter entitled: 'Dowsing'. He stared out of the window. The storm had blown itself out now and the sun was bright upon the pane, but all he saw was darkness. He thought of Ella. Sweet, gentle Ella. Where was she? What had they done to her? How would he live with himself if they killed her?

'It's got some photographs of pendulums,' Billy was saying. Fin looked back and saw his friend leafing through the book again. 'There, see?' said Billy. 'Loads of different types.'

Fin forced himself to look at the page. There were several photographs, each with a different pendulum. Billy chimed in again. 'You can make 'em out of anything. A ring, a key, a stone, or whatever you want.'

Fin clenched his hands, his teeth. He knew he was losing control and if he wasn't careful, he'd blurt out what had happened. He desperately wanted to go but he knew he couldn't leave Billy so soon. He'd only been here a short while and it would look suspicious.

'So what's this stuff got to do with finding things?' he made himself say.

'Well, you ask the pendulum questions and it gives you answers. Look, let's make one.'

'I haven't got time—'

'It won't take a moment.' Billy was already crawling over the bed to one of the cupboards on the far side. He pulled open the door and a dictionary fell out, followed by a half-eaten sandwich and some chess pieces. He ignored them, took something from one of the cupboard shelves, and closed the door again.

'Right, hold this.' He passed a small key to Fin. 'OK—string.' He sprawled over Fin and reached for the top drawer of the bedside cabinet.

'Hurry up,' said Fin, groaning under Billy's weight.

Billy rummaged in the drawer, then closed it and sat upright again. In his hand were a pair of scissors and a piece of string.

'Right, give us the key.'

Fin handed it over. Billy threaded the string through the hole in the key and tied a knot, then cut the string to just a few inches in length.

'It might be too long or too short. You have to experiment.'

'How come you know so much about this?'

'I had a go after I bought the book.'

'Did it work?'

'I wasn't very good at it. Apparently, anyone can dowse but some people have more of a knack than others. I'm not much good. But maybe I didn't stick at it long enough. I sort of got bored after a while.'

Surprise, surprise, Fin thought, but he said nothing. Billy went on.

'You hold the end of the string like this—OK?— and let the pendulum hang down. Then you wait to see which way it moves. It can go clockwise or anticlockwise, or in a straight line. You have to teach it to mean things. It's different for each person. I was trying to teach it to go clockwise for yes and anticlockwise for no.'

'You mean, you ask it questions and it moves?'

'It's supposed to. When you get the hang of it.'

'But you'd be moving it with your hand . . . I mean . . . the way you want it to go.'

'Not if you do it properly. And if you want to make it move, you don't have to use your hand anyway. You just move your eyes.'

'Never.'

'You do. Look.'

Billy held the string in his right hand and steadied the key with his left until it was still. 'Now, then. Tell me which way you want it to go.'

'Clockwise.'

Billy said nothing and simply stared at the pendulum. A few moments later it was gyrating— clockwise.

'You're moving it with your hand,' said Fin.

'I'm not. Look.'

Fin watched as closely as he could but saw no movement in Billy's arm or hand.

'Make it go anticlockwise,' he said.

He studied his friend closely. Billy was sitting rigidly still, as though determined not to move a muscle, yet the clockwise motion of the key was easing. A moment later it was moving again— anticlockwise.

'I can make it go straight, too,' said Billy. 'Forward and back or side to side.' He quickly obliged. 'See? It's easy. You try.'

'I can't do it.'

'You can. Anyone can do it. Just hold the pendulum still, then focus on it and let your eyes move in the direction you want. The pendulum will follow.'

Fin took the pendulum and held the end of the string. It felt somehow disloyal to Ella to be messing about like this when he should be out trying to do something to help her, yet he had started this with his own questioning, and there was something strangely compelling about the way the pendulum moved.

He made sure the key was still, then, keeping his eyes focused upon it, let them move clockwise. Surely the pendulum wouldn't respond. It had to be a trick that Billy had picked up somewhere; but the key soon started to move, gently at first, then with more vigour. After only a short time it was rotating clockwise.

'Told you,' said Billy. 'It's going better for you than it did for me. Make it go the other way.'

And it proved to be just as easy. Whichever way

51

he moved his eyes, the pendulum soon followed. But that in itself took away all his hopes. He reached out and stopped the motion of the key, and handed it back to Billy.

'You can't trust something you can move so easily. How can it give you a true answer if you can make it do what you want? You say is it OK to miss homework and it's bound to say yes. You'd make it say yes.'

'But you don't do that,' said Billy. 'You have to train it to mean yes one way and no the other, then, when you use it, you have to clear your mind, not force your wishes on it. You have to be sort of neutral when you ask it questions. It does work. I mean, read that chapter. It's full of stories.'

Billy held the book out to him. Fin shrugged and took it, though there seemed little point.

'Do you want to take the pendulum?' said Billy. 'I don't need the key. I can't remember what it's for.'

'No, it's all right. Look, I've got to go. I'll see you this afternoon.'

'OK.' Billy grinned at him. 'Hope your dad's going to let me take the wheel. I mean, there's no way I'm going out in a quality boat like that without having a go at the controls.'

'I expect he will,' said Fin. He stood up and Billy's grin faded.

'Fin?'

'Yeah?'

'You sure you're OK? You look like shit.'

'I'm fine,' he said.

He wasn't fine. He knew he was close to breaking point. He left Billy's house and made his way towards the village square. He didn't want to come this way but he didn't want to go home either. There was nowhere he wanted to be except where Ella was. He reached the village square and stood there, uncertain what to do.

Go home, he told himself. Go home. There's no point wandering about. Try and do something, anything. He turned and started to run back down the slope. A voice called after him. 'Fin?'

He stopped and looked round. It was Mrs Wilder from the shop. She held up a piece of newspaper. 'I cut this out for Ella. It's a report from the County Show. Have you got it already? I saved it just in case you'd missed it.'

'We've . . . we've got it. Thanks.'

'She did well, didn't she?'

'Yes.'

'And Angie.'

'Yes, she . . . they . . . I mean . . . ' He looked away. 'Sorry, I've got to go.'

He hurried to the bottom of the hill and started the climb towards Polvellan. Everywhere he looked now he saw darkness. It was like a mist above him, around him, inside him. He squeezed the book Billy had lent him and started to hate himself. He should never have taken it. He should never have sat playing games with Billy while Ella was in distress—a distress that he had caused and did not dare imagine.

He started to run again. He had to run. Perhaps if he ran fast enough, he could speed up the day, speed up time, so that tomorrow would come, and the kidnapper would phone, and they would give him the money, and Ella would come home. But time moved no faster. All that moved was his pain, like a shadow that would not let him go. He reached Polvellan and stopped by the gate, gasping for breath. Over in the paddock he saw Mum exercising Biscuit with Sam watching from behind the fence. Even from here he could see the anguish in her face. She was trying to hide it, trying to keep busy, trying not to worry Sam, but he knew what she was feeling. He ran over to the front door. He could not think even of Mum right now. He had to be by himself. He let himself in, tore up to his room, and threw himself on the bed.

7

Ella pressed herself against the wall. The boy had appeared in the entrance to the chamber, the sunlight catching him as it filtered through the gaps in the rock. He was still in his oilskins and had a plastic carrier bag in each hand. He stepped forward and stopped a few feet from her.

She pulled the blankets tightly around her and looked up at him, trembling. The face wasn't hard—there was even a gentleness about the mouth—but the sheer size of him terrified her, and there was anger in him, too: deep, dangerous anger. She felt as small and as frail as a baby. He put the bags down and started to take off his oilskins.

She slid down the wall away from him, still clutching the blankets. He made no effort to stop her. She reached the food boxes and pulled them across in front of her. The boy said nothing and continued to strip off his oilskins. She saw a scruffy sweater and jeans underneath, both stained and damp, and the collar and cuffs of a faded blue shirt. He dropped the oilskins to the floor and walked towards her, then slowly bent down.

'No!' she screamed.

But he was only checking the contents of the food boxes. He straightened up, fetched the carrier bags and emptied them out in front of her. It was more of the same: sandwich packs, bottles of mineral water, fruit and loo rolls, but he hadn't bought these from Dad's superstore. She could see from the labels. This stuff came from the garage shop just outside Trevally.

He stacked the supplies in the box, opened one of the sandwich packs and slumped to the ground a few feet from her, his back against the wall, and started eating. She watched uneasily. Anger still played round his face but now she sensed something else, too, something even deeper than anger. It was pain. Dark inner pain, twisting and torturing his mind before her eyes. For all his reckless confidence, this boy was in torment. She spoke.

'What are you going to do with me?'

He didn't answer, didn't stop eating, didn't glance her way. He reached for one of the bottles of mineral water, drank a little, then poured some into the cup of his hand and splashed it over his face. He finished the sandwiches, pulled out another pack and emptied that, too, then poked round in the box and picked out an apple.

She wished he would speak. She was chilled by his size, his strength, his obvious hatred of her, but this silence was almost as bad. She stared towards the tunnel. One dash and she'd be in it. The boy wasn't blocking her way. She might even make it down to the water. But what was the point? She'd never have time to get away in the boat before he caught her, and what would he do to her for trying to escape? She steeled herself and spoke again.

'Is it about money?'

Still no answer, only the crunching sound as he bit into the apple. She was desperate for him to speak now but he acted as though he wanted to block her from his mind. He finished the apple and threw the core to the side, then rested his head against the wall and closed his eyes. She did not try to speak again. He clearly had no intention of talking and further questions might provoke him to violence. At the moment he seemed to want only to sleep. She watched in case this were some ploy but his eyes remained closed and after a while his head rolled to the side. She saw his huge chest moving as he breathed.

She went on watching, still wary of him. No doubt he was exhausted after rowing through the storm but this might equally be a test to see whether she would make a dash for it; and then he would pounce. She waited and waited. More sunlight broke into the chamber through the gaps in the wall. She looked back at the boy, then slowly stood up. He did not stir. She crept as far as the top of the tunnel, held her breath and turned; his eyes were still closed. She hurried down the passageway.

Her spirit sank the moment she reached the cave. No wonder the boy felt relaxed enough to sleep. He'd pulled the dinghy clear of the water into the mouth of the tunnel and run a chain under the thwart through a ring-bolt in the wall that she hadn't seen before and back again. The ends were joined with a padlock. She felt a rush of disappointment. She hadn't expected an easy escape but suddenly, just for a moment, it had almost seemed possible. She squeezed past the dinghy and stepped out onto the flat rock that served as a landing stage.

The water was calm now and it was hard to believe there had been a storm. She sat down on the rock and stared out through the entrance to the cave. The sky was a deep blue and she could see gulls flying past. She wondered what time it was. Close to midday probably. Half a mile out the sun was brightening the rocky surfaces of the islands. She saw a boat heading towards them and jumped up to wave, but quickly sat down again. Nobody would see her in here.

She stayed on the rock for what felt like an hour or more, unwilling to go back to the chamber but knowing, as the minutes passed, that she would have to return soon. It might be dangerous to stay longer with the boy festering as he was with fury. If he woke and found her gone, he might do something terrible to her. She forced herself to climb back up the tunnel to the chamber. He was still slumped against the wall, his head rolled to the side, his eyes closed. She crept back to the blankets, sat down and pulled them round her, then gave a start.

His head had turned. He was watching her and there was something in his eyes that made her suspect he'd been awake all along, had even let her go down so that she would know she couldn't escape. She saw the anger and the pain burning in his face again. It was like a fire consuming him. He stood up and moved towards her. She pulled the blankets up to her neck. He stood over her, scowling, then knelt down and stretched a hand towards her face.

'No.' She twisted her head away. 'Please.'

He caught her by the hair.

'Please,' she said. 'Please no.'

He didn't let go, didn't move back. His face was only inches from hers, his cheeks twitching, his mouth tight. She looked into his eyes and saw his rage rolling over her in black waves; and deep inside him she sensed a desperate urge to kill. She started to whimper, to shake. He watched, still glaring at her, then suddenly, with a snarl, he let go of her hair and flicked it hard so that it flew to the side. She huddled into a ball, moaning, but he simply turned away, picked up his oilskins and disappeared down the tunnel.

Fin sat up on the bed, his eyes still wet from crying. Downstairs he could hear Mum talking to someone in the hall, then he caught the sound of Sam's voice. He quickly wiped his eyes with his sleeve. They mustn't see him like this.

'Fin?' Mum called up the stairs. 'Are you back?'

She sounded so tense, so vulnerable, so unlike her normal self. He stood up, opened the door and called back: 'Yes.'

'Lunch about half twelve.'

'OK.'

He closed the door and his eye fell on Billy's book. He picked it up somewhat reluctantly and skimmed through the chapter on dowsing, murmuring the section headings aloud: 'Finding Water . . . Finding Objects . . . Finding . . . ' He stopped, staring down at the page. 'Finding Missing Persons.'

He read the section once, then again, then the whole chapter. Soon he was devouring as much of the book as he could. From downstairs came clattering sounds in the kitchen but he read on greedily, almost dreading the call for lunch. When he'd taken in as much as he could, he put the book down and sat there, thinking hard; then he stood up and walked through to Ella's room.

Tears broke into his eyes again the moment he entered. He took a deep breath and walked over to the dressing table. There was her little jewellery box, the one she bought last year when Mum and Dad took them all to London. He opened it and took out the gold ring Nan gave her just before she died, then he picked up the hairbrush and unravelled one of the long golden strands of hair.

It looked so delicate and more gold than he ever remembered noticing when she was here, though not as deep a gold as the ring; and it seemed to him suddenly that only now did he realize just how beautiful Ella was. He stood there for a moment, thinking of her, seeing her face in his mind, almost hearing her voice calling to him. Then he remembered the book and what he had come to do.

'Come on,' he muttered to himself. 'Get on with it. You've done enough damage already and now you're wasting time as well.'

He hurried back to his room, sat on the bed, and tied the ring to the end of the hair.

'Please hold,' he murmured. 'Please don't break.'

But the hair showed no sign of breaking. Indeed, it seemed more than comfortable supporting the ring. He held the other end of the hair between his thumb and forefinger, just as he had held the string and the key at Billy's house, then put his other hand around the ring to keep it still.

Command the pendulum, the book said. Teach it yes and no. Train it.

He thought of how his eyes had made the pendulum move at Billy's house.

'Go clockwise for yes,' he murmured, and he moved his eyes clockwise. Sure enough, just as before, the pendulum started to move clockwise. 'This is yes,' he said, remembering the instructions in the book. 'This is yes. This is yes.'

The ring was moving almost violently now. He stopped it with his left hand. It hung there, motionless, as though waiting for his next command.

'Go anticlockwise for no,' he said, and he moved his eyes that way; and once again the pendulum started to move, this time anticlockwise. 'This is no,' he said. 'This is no. This is no.'

He watched it for a moment, fascinated. There was something magical about the hair and the ring moving together. He stopped the pendulum again. Perhaps he should try a test run now and see if it worked. He studied the book again. Ask questions that require yes-no answers, it said. He held the pendulum before him and spoke to it. 'Is Teddy in this room?'

The pendulum remained still.

'Is Teddy in this room?'

No movement.

This was stupid. It wasn't going to work. He knew Teddy wasn't here but the pendulum wasn't saying anything at all. He heard more clattering sounds in the kitchen and knew that Mum would be calling up any moment. He spoke to the pendulum again.

'Is Teddy in this room?'

Still nothing. He remembered something he had read in the book about how it sometimes helps to have the pendulum swinging forward and back before asking it a question. He started the pendulum moving with his hand.

'Is Teddy in this room?'

No response.

'Is Teddy in this room?'

'He's here,' said a voice.

He looked up and saw Sam standing in the doorway, holding Teddy.

'What's that?' said Sam, looking at the strange ring attached to the hair.

'A pendulum.'

'What's a pendlam? Is it magic?'

Fin remembered the title of the book. 'It's supposed to be.'

'What's it do?'

'You ask it questions and it tells you things. But you have to know how to use it. Some people can't.' He frowned. 'I can't.'

'Let me do it.'

Fin hesitated, unwilling to involve Sam in this; but it couldn't do any harm.

'Come here, then, Sammy.'

Sam came over and sat with him on the bed.

'You hold it like this,' said Fin. 'Then you ask it questions. It works different ways for different people. But some people find it goes clockwise—'

'What's clockwise?'

'Like this.' Fin spun the pendulum. 'That's clockwise, see? The same way a clock moves.'

'Your clock doesn't go like that.'

'It's digital, that's why. But the one in the hall—'

'The gran'father clock.'

'Good boy. The grandfather clock. That's got a normal clockface and if you look at the hands, you'll see they go clockwise. The way this pendulum's going.'

'It's stopped.'

'Well, OK.' Fin spun it again. 'Now it's going,

right? That's clockwise.' He stopped it and spun it the other way. 'And that's called anticlockwise. Like I say, sometimes it spins one way, sometimes the other. The book says some people find that clockwise means yes and anticlockwise means no. So they can ask it questions and it gives answers. Only, like I say, it doesn't seem to work for everyone.'

Sam held out his hand. 'Let me.'

'You'll only be upset if it doesn't work for you.'

'But it might work for me.'

Fin handed it over. Sam took it and held it by the end of the thread of hair. The pendulum hung motionless.

'Ask it a question,' Sam said.

Fin shrugged. This was going to end in disaster. Sam was bound to be disappointed when it didn't work.

'Ask it a question,' said Sam again.

'I think you have to ask the questions,' said Fin, playing for time.

'What question shall I ask it?'

'Oh, I don't know.' Fin thought for a moment. 'Ask it if Daddy's in the house.'

'Is Daddy in the house?' Sam's voice sounded strangely grave and his eyes were fixed on the pendulum. At once it started to move in a clockwise direction, steadily picking up speed. Sam looked round in triumph. 'See?'

'You're moving it.'

'I'm not!'

'You are.' Fin folded his arms. 'And if clockwise means yes, it's wrong anyway because Daddy's not back yet.'

63

'He is. He just came in. And I'm not moving it. It's moving itself.'

Fin watched. It did seem as though the pendulum had moved of its own accord, and it had started from a stationary position. Fin reached out, stopped the ring and released it again.

'Ask it another question,' he said.

'What question?'

'Hang on a moment while I think of one.'

But Sam spoke first, in the same earnest voice, his eyes still on the pendulum.

'Is Ella alive?'

Fin sat up with a start. The question seemed to pierce him like a javelin, but already the pendulum was moving again, clockwise as before. He stared at it. It couldn't mean anything, however much he wanted it to. Probably the pendulum would always move clockwise for Sam. He tried to think of a silly question.

'Ask the pendulum if Mummy's a man.'

Sam looked at him gravely.

'But Mummy's a woman.'

'Just ask it.'

'Is Mummy a man?' said Sam in the same respectful voice to the pendulum.

The ring started to move, anticlockwise. Fin watched, still unconvinced. Billy had shown him how easy it was to make the pendulum move the way you wanted, yet Sam knew nothing of that. He was simply asking the questions and the pendulum was answering, or so it seemed. He tried to think of sterner tests.

'Ask the pendulum if Daddy's in the drawing room.'

'Is Daddy in the drawing room?'

No, said the pendulum.

'Ask it different rooms.'

'Is Daddy in the sitting room?' said Sam.

No.

'Is Daddy in the kitchen?'

No.

'Is Daddy in the hall?'

And so it went on, no to every room in the house. Sam looked round at him.

'But Daddy's in the house. I saw him.'

'Maybe he's gone into the garden. Ask the pendulum.'

'Is Daddy in the garden?'

No.

'Sammy, ask it again if Daddy's in the house.'

'Is Daddy in the house?'

The pendulum moved clockwise at once. Fin reached out and stopped the ring, and took the pendulum from Sam.

'It's a bit funny, this pendulum. It doesn't always give the right answers. We've mentioned every room and it says Daddy's not there but it's still telling us he's in the house. Don't be upset, Sammy. You've done very well.'

Mum called up the stairs again. 'Boys! Come and eat!'

'Come on, Sammy,' said Fin. 'Now we'll find out where Daddy is.'

They ran to the top of the stairs and looked down but there was no sign of Dad. Hand in hand they made their way to the foot of the stairs where Mum was waiting for them.

'Have either of you seen your father?' she said.

'I'm in here,' came Dad's voice from the sitting room. Fin led the way through and saw the door to the secret passageway open. A moment later Dad appeared, carrying a torch. 'I was just looking round in case there were any clues,' he said.

'Why in there?' said Mum.

'The door wasn't closed properly. I just noticed it. It was slightly ajar. Someone's been in there. I checked the other end by the kitchen but that was shut.' He looked at Fin. 'Have you been in there over the last couple of days?'

'No.'

'Sam?'

It seemed pointless asking Sam as he couldn't reach the catch but he shook his head anyway.

'Well, somebody has,' said Dad. 'I just thought Ella might have gone in there to hide or something. Anyway, I didn't see anything.' He closed the door.

Fin checked to see where Sam was and saw him crawling under the table to pick up his model car. He lowered his voice. 'Dad, did you see Mr Treadaway at the bank?'

'You don't need to worry about that.'

'But did you? I mean, did you fix everything?'

'Yes. The money'll be ready for collection in the morning.'

'And was he a bit funny when you told him what you wanted?'

'Why should he be? It's none of his business what I do with my money.' He glanced at Mum. 'I don't want any lunch,' he said and walked, frowning, out into the hall. A few moments later Fin heard the back door open and close. Mum pursed her lips.

'Well, you and Sam are going to have lunch,'

she said. 'I've cooked it and somebody's going to eat it.'

Sam came back with his model car and Fin took him by the hand again and walked with him through to the dining room. But he ate and said little. His mind was now racing. The secret passageway was the one part of the house they had forgotten to ask the pendulum about. He felt in his pocket for the ring and held it tight.

8

'Now this is what I call a boat,' said Billy.

Fin leaned back on the foredeck as *Free Spirit* powered out of the cove towards the open sea. This was the last place he wanted to be right now. He'd rather have stayed at home with Mum and Sam and Mrs Meade than come out here just to make things look 'normal'. Billy gabbled on excitedly.

'She's absolutely beautiful. What are we talking about, forty foot?'

'Forty-five.'

'Brand new?'

'Yes.'

'I mean brand spanking new?'

'I just said.'

'Dad's dead jealous. I mean, I know he acts like he prefers sailing boats and stuff but this is something else.'

Fin said nothing. He knew Mr Meade was jealous of Dad but he couldn't think of that now. All he could think of was Ella and Sam and the pendulum; and Mum. She was acting brave in front of Sam but it was obvious she was close to despair. He wished Dad would hold her more. Angie drifted over to them, looking as petulant as she'd been earlier, and sat with them on the foredeck.

'I still can't understand why Ella never said anything. It's not like her.'

'Give it a rest, Angie,' said Billy.

She pouted at him and looked at Fin. 'Where are we going?'

'Don't think we're going anywhere,' said Fin. 'Think we're just going to motor around.'

'Can we go to the islands?'

'What for?' said Billy.

'I haven't been there for ages.'

'Who wants to?' Billy wrinkled his nose. 'Three little islands with nothing on them but bird-shit?'

'I'd still like to see them.'

'Well, it looks like we're heading out to sea so hard luck.'

Fin stood up, in no mood to hear Billy and Angie bickering, and joined Dad and Mr Meade in the wheelhouse. Mr Meade gave him a nod.

'Like the new boat, Fin?'

'Yeah, it's great.'

'Just wish I could get your dad to buy a nice new car from my showroom to go with it.' Mr Meade looked up at the Pengrig headland to starboard. 'And I haven't given up on persuading him to join the Save-the-Lighthouse campaign either.'

'I keep telling you,' said Dad. 'I'm not interested. I've got too much on.'

'But you could really help. The lighthouse can be saved but nothing's been done apart from fencing it off. Another big storm and it'll topple. You're exactly the kind of person with enough influence to make a difference.'

'Enough money, more like,' said Dad.

'Well, that, too, but it's in a good cause. And you can't say you don't care about the lighthouse. What about those sketches you did of it? The ones hanging up in your hall.'

'What about them?'

'Well, you must have cared about the lighthouse when you drew those.'

'That was ten years ago.'

Fin had heard this conversation too often to want to hear it again. 'Dad,' he said, 'can we go and have a look at the islands?'

'What for? There's nothing to see now the nesting birds have gone.'

'I think Angie wants to have a look at them.'

'All right. But I don't want to go ashore.'

'OK.' Fin thought for a moment. 'Have you got the ship-to-shore radio working?'

'No.'

'Can I borrow your mobile, then?'

'What for?'

'I want to speak to Mum.'

'What about?'

'I just want to ask her something.'

Dad handed him the phone.

'What's wrong with the ship-to-shore radio?' said Mr Meade.

'Playing up,' said Dad. 'Bad battery lead, I think, or maybe the aerial connection. I haven't had time to look at it.'

Fin left them talking and made his way to the stern of the boat. The Pengrig headland was on the starboard beam now and he could see the mouth of the cave before him. He switched on the mobile and dialled the number.

'Hello?' said Mum.

'It's me.'

'Fin?'

'Yeah.'

'Where are you? On the boat?'

'Yeah.'

'Is everything all right?'

'Yeah.' He paused, his eyes on the old lighthouse. 'Well . . . no.'

There was a silence, then Mum spoke again. 'Darling?'

'Yeah?'

'I know how you're feeling.'

'And I know how you're feeling,' he said.

'You do?'

'Yeah. That's why I rang.'

She gave a long sigh. 'I'm OK, Fin,' she said.

'You're not. You sound terrible.'

'Do I?' She gave another sigh. 'You're right—I'm worried sick about Ella. I'm just . . . so scared for her. But, Fin, listen—I'll cope with this somehow. I'll get through it. And you must do the same. Don't worry about me. Worry about yourself instead. Get yourself right.'

'I feel so bad.'

'I know you do but, darling, remember, whatever we're feeling, Ella's feeling it worse. We've got to be strong and stick together or we won't be able to help her.'

'Has anyone rung?'

'No.'

'Is Sammy all right?'

'He's out in the garden with Mrs Meade.'

'But is he all right?'

'He's acting a bit strange but I suppose that's to be expected.'

They were clear of Pengrig now and Fin could see Dad turning the wheel to head down the coast. 'I'd better go,' he said.

'Fin?'

'Yeah?'

'Don't keep crucifying yourself.'

'It was my fault. I went out. I left her.'

'I know but you've got to put that behind you now.'

He didn't answer.

'Fin, are you listening?'

'Yeah.'

'You've got to put that behind you. We've all slipped up over things. We've all made mistakes. You've got to try and move on from it, OK?'

'Suppose so.'

'I'll see you soon.'

'OK.'

He rang off, feeling no better either about Mum or himself. The islands were dead ahead now. He wandered back to the wheelhouse, handed Dad the phone, and rejoined Billy and Angie on the foredeck. She looked round at him. 'Is this your doing?'

'What do you mean?'

'Us going to the islands.'

'Maybe.'

'Thanks.'

He shrugged. 'Fancied a trip there myself.'

Not that he did. He had no more time for the islands than Billy. He couldn't understand why tourists wanted to make boat trips there. In the nesting season there was plenty of bird life but this time of year there were only gulls hanging round. The two smaller islands were close now and he tried to show interest.

But it was no good. Rocky islands held no fascination. Dad steered the boat between them and headed for the largest of the three. Fin watched it draw closer. At least this one was worth landing on. There was a protected inlet at the southern end with a jetty for the tourist boats and although, like the others, the island consisted only of rocks, it was just about large enough for a ramble, though at two hundred yards from end to end, it was a pretty short one.

Dad slowed down as they cruised in. There were several gulls on the island but most of the rocks were bare. Angie watched for a moment, then suddenly turned to Billy. 'What was it Dad said sailors used to call the islands?'

'The Furies,' he said.

'What for?'

'What for?' Billy stared at her. 'It's obvious.'

'Not to me, it's not.'

'They're named after the Furies. You know, from classical mythology.' Angie's face remained blank. Billy groaned. 'You know about the Furies?'

'No.'

'God, you're ignorant.'

'I'm not!'

'You are. You're thick. Everyone knows who the Furies were.'

'Well, I don't.'

'Like I say, you're thick.'

Fin gave Billy a prod. 'I don't know who they were either.'

'Well, you're both dummies.' Billy studied the island for a moment. 'The Furies were women. There were three of them. Three islands, three women. Get it? They were goddesses of vengeance. Or something like that.'

'Don't tell me,' said Fin. 'You've got a book about them in your room.'

'Yeah. It's got some pictures, too. Dead gruesome.' He saw Mr Meade wandering forward to join them. 'Dad? Who were the Furies?'

'The Furies?' Mr Meade pulled a horror-film face and advanced upon them, hands outstretched like claws. 'Three horrible old hags, instruments of retribution. They had snakes for hair and wings and gory eyes and they punished people for wrongdoing. If you were guilty of a crime, especially a crime within the family, the Furies drove you insane.'

'These islands would drive me insane,' said Billy. 'I'd go mad from sheer boredom.'

'They're much more dangerous than that,' said Mr Meade. 'More boats have foundered on these rocks over the centuries than we'll ever know about. The coastline round here's a graveyard. The islands are well named.'

Billy threw a glance at Fin. 'See? Even the gaffer knows who the Furies were.'

Fin looked away, his mind not on fearsome old women, but on Ella and Sam, and what he had to do.

It was half past five by the time they made it back to the house. Fin hurried up to his room, glad to be free of company. Billy and Angie had gone but Mr and

Mrs Meade were still hanging around in the garden, talking to Mum and Dad.

He checked Billy's book again, then went to the big cabinet in Dad's study and opened the drawer where the maps were kept. He pulled them out, dumped them on the bed in his room, and went to look for Sam. He was coming up the stairs, Teddy in one hand and his model car in the other.

'All right, Sammy?'

Sam stopped just below the top and looked up at him. He still found stairs a little difficult. Fin stepped forward.

'I can do it myself,' said Sam.

Fin grabbed him round the waist and hauled him over his shoulder. 'You sure about that, monster?'

Sam squealed with pleasure. 'I'm not a monster!'

'Who says?'

'Me.'

'Oh, yeah?' Fin carried him into the bedroom, pushed the maps onto the floor, and dangled him over the bed, then let him fall gently onto his bottom. Sam bounced up and down on the mattress, still clinging to Teddy and the model car, then he stopped and peered over the edge of the bed.

'What's that?' he said.

'Maps, Sammy.' Fin picked up the route map of the British Isles and started to open it. 'Move to the side a bit, can you? I want to spread it out on the bed. Sit on the pillow if you want.'

Sam dropped Teddy and the model car to the floor and sat on the pillow, watching with interest. Fin spread out the map and smoothed it with his hand.

'See that word?' he said, pointing. Sam stared at it. Fin put his finger on the first letter. 'M,' he said, and he read on, pointing to each letter as it came: 'M-A-N-C-H-E-S-T-E-R. Manchester. Where Daddy was born.'

'What's it like?'

'Don't know. Never been there. You'll have to ask Daddy. It's supposed to rain a lot. Don't know much else about it.'

'Where's Mummy born?'

'Other end of the country. Hang on.' He studied the bottom of the map. 'Down here somewhere. There you go. R-A-M-S-G-A-T-E. Ramsgate.'

Sam watched intently. 'But what do you want the map for?'

Fin hesitated. It still didn't seem right involving Sam in this but he'd been so good with the pendulum before, and maybe the fact that he couldn't read would help him keep his mind clear, like the book said you were supposed to.

'Sammy, I want to use the map and the pendulum to see if we can find out where Ella is. But I don't want to tell Mummy and Daddy. Not yet. They might think it's silly and anyway, it might not work.'

'You said it's magic so it must work.'

'Well, maybe it is but not everyone knows how the spell works so you mustn't be disappointed if you can't do it. Still, you did pretty well before lunch.'

'Give me the pendlam.'

'OK.' Fin still felt uneasy but he handed Sam the pendulum. The golden hair seemed bright as the late afternoon sun caught it through the window. 'Now, then, Sammy, it's a bit different to what we did this morning. The book says you have to hold the pendulum in one hand and then move your other hand all over the map with your finger pointing down—like this, OK?—and you keep asking the pendulum to show you where she is. Just say: Show me where Ella is.'

'What's the pendlam going to do?'

'It's supposed to spin round or something if your finger touches the spot where Ella is.'

'Let's start!'

'OK. We'll use this map first and see if she's in the British Isles.' He frowned and murmured to himself: 'I bloody hope she is.'

Sam held the pendulum in his right hand and traced the index finger of his left hand over the map. 'Show me where Ella is,' he said to the pendulum. 'Show me where Ella is.'

The pendulum remained still but Fin expected no response: Sam's finger was travelling through Edinburgh and she surely wasn't up there. It moved on through Stirling, Perth, Dundee . . .

He glanced down at Cornwall, wishing Sam would try down there, but he knew it was best not to coax the little boy. Let him move the pendulum where he wanted, at least to begin with.

'Show me where Ella is. Show me where Ella is.'

The finger was moving, down, down. Newcastle, Middlesborough, Scarborough, York . . .

Still no response from the pendulum.

'Show me where Ella is.'

Sheffield, Nottingham, Leicester, Peterborough . . .

The finger moved on, ever southwards, and still the pendulum hung motionless. Fin watched nervously. Outside the window Mr and Mrs Meade were still talking to Mum and Dad, their voices a murmur of words he could not catch; then he heard a goodbye and a moment later the click of the gate.

Mum and Dad talked for a while longer, then their voices faded away in the direction of the stable.

'Show me where Ella is.'

Sam's voice brought his mind back, but still there was no response from the pendulum. He was desperate now for Sam to move his finger over Cornwall. Down by the stable he heard a whinny from Biscuit, then a new voice calling from the lane. It sounded like old Mr Aldridge taking his dog for a walk. There was a brief exchange of words, then silence. He looked back at the pendulum. Nothing was happening and Sam's finger was miles from Cornwall.

'Sammy, why not try down this way?'

'I'll do it myself.'

'All right, Sammy.'

'Show me where Ella is.' Sam's voice sounded so strange now, just as it had done this morning. It was graver, deeper than his normal voice. Fin watched as the places passed beneath the finger, places whose names Sam could not read: Northampton, Coventry, Birmingham, Worcester . . .

Now he was moving west; and still the pendulum did not stir.

'Keep asking the question, Sammy.'

'I know what to do.'

'Sorry.'

'Show me where Ella is.'

Fin watched, yearning more than ever for Sam to move his finger down to Cornwall, but no, Sam was going to do it his own way. He was frowning now, his tongue out, as it always was when he was concentrating hard.

'Show me where Ella is.'

The pendulum did not respond. The finger moved on, slowly, slowly, Sam's face fiercely focused, strangely still, strangely old, his eyes like moist jewels. The pendulum hung still, without life, and the names passed on: Hereford, Gloucester, Bristol, Taunton . . .

'Show me where Ella is.'

Fin held his breath, his body tense. Sam's voice sounded so solemn now and there was a mesmeric stillness about him. The finger moved closer to Cornwall.

'Show me where Ella is.'

No response and the finger moved on. Sam had clearly worked out that the words in bold print were the bigger places and he was going only for these, even though he couldn't read them and wouldn't know that he was now pointing at Cornwall. He spoke suddenly.

'R.'

'What's that, Sammy?'

'R. Like Ramsgate.'

Fin looked down and saw where the finger was pointing.

'Redruth. Good boy. R-E-D-R-U-T-H.' He decided to risk another rebuke from Sam. 'Sammy, try moving your finger over this way. You haven't covered that bit yet.'

To his surprise Sam obliged and moved the finger towards the Newquay area.

'Show me where Ella is.'

Fin held his breath and watched, waited, prayed. Suddenly the pendulum spun clockwise. He sat up with a jerk and gave a whoop.

'She's in the area! Give me five, Sammy!'

Sam put the pendulum down and they clapped palms together.

'Right, Sammy, let's try something else.' Fin bundled the map onto the floor, too excited to fold it away properly, then hunted through the other maps.

'What are you doing?' said Sam.

'Looking for the local map. It's really detailed. We might be able to pinpoint exactly where she is.'

He found the map and spread it over the bed. 'Go on, Sammy. Same again.'

Sam picked up the pendulum and held it over the map. Fin pointed to the centre of Newquay. 'Why not start here, Sammy? See if she's in a house in Newquay.'

Sam looked round at him.

'All right, Sammy. I know. You'll do it yourself.'

Fin smiled but he was now elated. He stared at the pendulum, which only a moment ago had been spinning by some mysterious power. It was motionless again on its bright gold thread of hair, yet the power that had moved it once must surely move it again. Perhaps it was working even now. He studied Sam's face. As before, it was rigid with concentration.

'Show me where Ella is.'

The finger started to move, not through Newquay but through Trevally.

Fin's mouth fell open. It had to be coincidence. Sam could not read the name and would not understand the map markings. Yet of all the villages he had to choose from, he was moving his finger through their own: past the playing field, past the church, past the pub, across the square, down the hill, and now up the lane towards Polvellan.

It was as though Sam knew this was the road to their house. Yet he could not. He had never studied a map in his life. Perhaps he realized these lines represented a road; perhaps not. Whatever the reason, he was following the lane up to their house.

'Show me where Ella is.'

The finger moved on, the pendulum still hanging motionless, and continued past Polvellan and on towards the coastal path. Fin watched, wondering whether the finger would stop at the cliff-edge. Sam surely would not realize that the pale blue section meant the sea. But the finger stopped at the cliff-line, then moved on, right, along the coastal path. Fin glanced at Sam's face and saw beads of sweat running down his cheeks.

'You all right, Sammy?'

Sam didn't seem to hear him. The finger moved as before but more beads of sweat were appearing. Sam looked up suddenly and stared towards the corner of the room.

'I can't come!' he said.

Fin looked at him in alarm. 'Sammy? What's up?'

Sam didn't answer. He was still staring at the wall. Fin stared, too, but saw nothing, then he noticed the pendulum. It was spinning furiously and Sam's finger had pressed right through the map. But Sam saw none of this. His eyes were still staring towards the far wall. Suddenly he dropped the pendulum and scrambled off the bed.

'Sammy, what's wrong?'

Sam ran towards the door.

'Sammy, come back!'

But Sam did not stop. He tore out of the room

and down the landing towards the head of the stairs. Fin raced after him, caught him round the waist and hoisted him off the floor.

'Leave me alone!' screamed Sam. 'Leave me alone!'

'Sammy, easy.'

Sam didn't look at him. His eyes were flickering everywhere, his body twisting in Fin's arms as though he were straining for a glimpse of something. Suddenly he burst into tears.

'Easy, Sammy.' Fin stroked his head. 'I thought you were going to jump off the top of the stairs.'

Sam sobbed in his arms, his body suddenly limp. Fin hesitated, then put him down, but kept between him and the stairs. Sam looked up at him.

'I wasn't going to jump,' he said, still crying. 'That's naughty.'

'But what's wrong, Sammy?'

'She's gone.'

'Who?' Fin knelt down and looked him in the face. 'Who's gone?'

Sam looked away. 'It's a secret. I promised I wouldn't tell anyone except Teddy.'

'OK.' He pulled Sam to him. At first there was no response, then he felt Sam's arms slip round his back; and they hugged each other.

'I love you, Sammy.'

Sam was still snuffling but the worst seemed to be over. Fin stroked the back of the little boy's head. 'I won't tell anyone. I promise. OK?'

Sam looked at him and sniffed.

'Got a hankie?' said Fin.

Sam nodded and fumbled in one of his trouser pockets.

'It's not there,' he said, his eyes watering again.

'Let's have a look.' Fin felt in Sam's other pocket and eventually pulled out a crumpled handkerchief. 'There you go.' He reached out to wipe away the tears but Sam quickly took the handkerchief from him.

'I'll do it myself.'

'OK, Sammy.'

Fin smiled at him. The tension seemed to have gone for the moment but something was clearly wrong. Whatever this particular secret was, it had unsettled him badly. Fin hoped it would pass as quickly as it had come.

'All right now, Sammy?'

Sam was still wiping his face but he nodded. Fin gave him a soft punch on the arm.

'Come on, then. Give me five.'

And they clapped palms again.

'Let's go and get Teddy,' said Fin.

They fetched Teddy and the model car and Sam ran off to his room. Fin waited for a moment, listening, but all was well. Sam seemed to have calmed down but what had caused this outburst was still a mystery. His eye fell on the map on his bed. He bent over it and studied the spot where Sam's finger had pushed through.

It was the Pengrig lighthouse.

9

At dusk he took his torch and set off alone, up to the cliffs and the coastal path. He felt slightly guilty about lying to Mum and Dad and saying he was just going for a stroll into the village but even that had been hard enough to get Mum to agree to. She was so frightened of him leaving the house now, especially with the kidnappers out there and darkness coming on. But he'd insisted he'd be back soon, and he felt certain he would be. He surely wouldn't find anything at the Pengrig lighthouse.

Not Ella, anyway. How could the pendulum be right? The deserted lighthouse, perched like an eagle's nest on the crumbling cliff-head, was hardly the place to keep a hostage girl, yet the pendulum had clearly spun at that point and he knew he had to check just in case there was some clue.

He walked on, glad that the high winds of yesterday had died down. Below him the sea stretched away in an inky haze. The light was fading fast but he could just make out the three little islands offshore. Up to the right the new automatic lighthouse was throwing out its bright flashing signals but down by the cliff-head the tower of the old Pengrig looked gaunt and uninviting as dusk settled around it.

He studied the way the lantern craned over the sea: the leaning tower of Trevally, as Billy called it. It was only a matter of time before the whole thing fell, unless Mr Meade and his team managed to persuade the authorities to get it moved, which seemed unlikely.

He drew closer, thinking of Ella and that cocksure voice on the phone, and how he wished he could see the face that went with it. What would he do to that face, he wondered, if he had the chance? It almost frightened him to think of it. He reached the fence that had been put up to keep people away from the lighthouse and the edge of the cliff. The words on the notice were just visible in the fading light.

DANGER!
CLIFF AND LIGHTHOUSE VERY UNSTABLE.
DO NOT GO BEYOND THIS POINT.

He looked about him. There was no sign of anyone. He climbed over the fence and dropped onto the ground on the other side. He was trembling now. The chances of the cliff collapsing or the lighthouse falling at this precise moment were remote indeed and vandals had been into the lighthouse several times since it was fenced off, but he still felt uneasy. This was a creepy place and the sooner he was out of it, the better.

He walked up to the entrance and stopped in the unblocked doorway, his eyes darting around him, but there was no sign of anyone. He stepped inside and made his way towards the stairway. The place smelt mouldy and the wind he had thought absent on the way here now seemed to whistle around him. He started to climb. The stairway was cheerless and dark, and there was a chill that grew deeper as he drew higher. He reached the old lighthouse keeper's office and glanced round. It was growing darker and darker but he didn't want to switch on the torch in case someone were here and he gave himself away.

But there was no one on this floor. He stared round the room, dimly able to make out its features. The old wooden cabinets were still there, though the glass had been shattered, and the walls were paint-sprayed with graffiti. He walked over to the steep metal steps that led up to the lantern, and put his hand on the rail. Still no sound, apart from the whistling wind. Suddenly he wanted to call out. The gloom of this place felt oppressive and he wanted to run away but he knew he had to steel himself and go to the top. He gripped the rail and forced himself to climb.

But there was no one in the lantern. He glanced around the moment his head was through the opening but he was clearly alone. He climbed the last few steps and flicked on the torch, keeping the beam low. There was nothing here, just the metal legs that had once supported the lens and more graffiti, this time on the floor. The door to the balcony had been smashed and left hanging.

He looked through the opening and saw far below him the sea driving in to the base of the cliff. He felt his head swirl and stepped back. Nothing would persuade him to go out there and fortunately there was no need. Ella was not here.

The pendulum was wrong.

He switched off the torch and stared over the sea. It was turning black, like the sky. He looked for the islands and saw they had been swallowed in darkness. He made his way back to the ground floor and out through the doorway. It was good to be outside again. He felt vulnerable here. He hurried to the fence, climbed over it and ran for home.

At the fork in the track he stopped and looked towards the cove. There was nothing to see now that the light was gone, save the white of the surf as the sea rumbled in. He ran on down the lane and saw the figure of Mr Aldridge hobbling towards him with his dog.

'Hello, Mr Aldridge,' he called.

'Fin? That you?'

'Yes.'

They stopped.

'Sorry,' said Mr Aldridge. 'Didn't recognize you in the darkness. Buster, get down.'

'It's all right. He's fine.' Fin reached down and stroked the dog.

'What brings you this way?' said Mr Aldridge.

'Just walking.'

'Ella with you?'

'No.' He hoped Mr Aldridge would walk on soon. He was in no mood for conversation. Fortunately, neither was Mr Aldridge.

'I won't stop, Fin, if you don't mind. The old back's playing up again. It's a bugger, I'm telling you. Walking's the only thing that gives me any relief.' He whistled to the dog. 'Come on, boy. I'll be seeing you, Fin.' And he continued towards the cliffs.

Fin hurried on in the direction of the house, now anxious to be back. Mum would be worrying about him for sure. At last he saw the stone wall that bordered the garden, then the paddock and stable, and the lights of Polvellan. And, to his surprise, another figure, craning over the wall towards the house.

He stopped. The figure did not turn and seemed unaware of him in the darkness. He stole forward, keeping as low as he could and staying in the shadow, then he heard a voice from the other side of the wall.

'I've told you before. You're not to come here.'

He stiffened. It was his father's voice. He strained to see more. The figure was a man, a small man with a long coat. Even in the darkness he looked untidy and unkempt. Fin searched for a glimpse of Dad and caught him, half hidden by the bushes.

'Now get out of here,' Dad hissed. 'And I don't want you hanging round the house again.'

The man swayed on his feet for a moment and seemed to be considering what to do, then he gave a wheezy cough, pulled his coat round him and shuffled away down the hill towards the village. Fin watched him, then glanced over the wall again in time to see Dad disappear through the back door of the house. He crept towards the gate, his eye fixed on the figure retreating down the lane.

He thought of Dad's words: 'I've told you before. You're not to come here.'

What was going on? The simple answer was to ask Dad, yet there was something so shifty about this meeting by the wall. Suddenly he was hurrying down the hill. He had to follow this man and see where he went. He slipped down the lane as quietly as he could, glad that the darkness had deepened further. The man still seemed unaware of him and continued plodding down towards the bottom of the hill. Billy's house appeared on the right, the lights bright against the darkness—and the man stopped.

Fin froze, sensing that his presence had been detected, but the figure did not turn. Instead it lurched over to the other side of the lane and stopped by the stile to the public footpath. Fin narrowed his eyes and watched. The man put a hand on the stile to steady himself, then reached into one of the pockets of his coat. Out came a bottle, the man's head tipped back and seemed to stay back for ages, then there was a long sigh and the bottle returned to the pocket; and the man staggered on towards the slope that led up to the square.

Fin followed, feeling slightly less worried. He knew he could outrun an old drunk if the man turned and came for him, but the thought of Dad having dealings with someone like this bothered him even more now. The man continued to the square and stopped outside the shop, swaying on his feet, then vanished round the side of the building. Fin ran up and peered into the square. The tramp had passed the pub and the war memorial and was trudging down the Newquay road. Fin heard the sound of an engine and looked round.

A Land Rover roared into the square and turned off down the same road. The man held out a thumb. It was ignored and he walked on. Fin stroked his chin and stared at the man's retreating back. It was a long hike to Newquay and would probably feel even longer to a drunk—if that was where he was going. Maybe he would turn off to one of the other villages. Maybe he'd spend the night in a field. Fin frowned. It made no sense, Dad knowing a man like this. But then nothing made sense any more.

He ran back to Polvellan to find Mum and Dad outside the gate, both holding torches. Dad saw him coming and flashed a beam over him.

'Fin?'

'Yes.'

'Where the hell have you been?'

But Mum called out before he could answer.

'Is Sam with you?'

'Sam?'

She rushed up and seized him by the arm. He felt her hand shaking.

'Is he with you?' She was looking frantically over his shoulder, searching the lane behind him. 'Please say he's with you.'

'He's not with me.'

'Oh, God! I was praying he would be.'

'The last time I saw him he was asleep in his room.'

Dad hurried forward. 'Well, he's gone missing again.' He shot a glance at Mum. 'We'll search the fields round the house first. If we don't find him, we'll try the coastal path. He might just have gone up there again.'

Without a word she let go of Fin's arm and raced off up the lane. Fin turned to follow but Dad put a hand on his shoulder and stopped him.

'You'd better stay here in case he turns up. Have another look round the house.'

'OK.'

'Check the garden, too.'

And he sprinted off after Mum. Fin switched on his own torch, ran down to the stable and stopped outside.

'Sammy? You in there?'

He heard a snort from Biscuit but nothing else.

'Sammy, if this is a game, can you stop playing and come out?'

No answer. He checked the stable anyway but Sam was not there. He ran down to the paddock and into the orchard. Still no sign. He dashed back to the house. The lights were on but the place felt strangely dark. He searched all the downstairs rooms, even the secret passageway. No Sam. He tore upstairs and looked around him.

The lights were on here, too, and the bedroom doors all open. He walked down, his eyes searching. Nothing, and no clues that he could see. He stopped outside Sam's room and looked in. The door to the cupboard was open—it was the first place Mum and Dad would have looked—but Sam was not there.

He walked into Ella's room and stopped by the window. Outside all was black. He felt panic rising within him and suddenly he was shrieking, shrieking at the top of his voice. It was a mad, wordless yell and the sound of it terrified him, but he went on shrieking, unable to stop, until his throat resisted and he fell silent. He clapped a hand to his face and screwed his eyes tight; and into his mind came the sound of the kidnapper's voice, taunting him.

You'll never find her. You'll never find her.

'Go away!' he bellowed.

And now you've lost your little brother too.

'Go away! Go away! Go away!'

The doorbell rang. He tensed, his mind still in turmoil; it rang again and this time roused him to action. He darted out of Ella's room and leapt down the stairs in great bounds. Mr Aldridge was standing on the doorstep, a small figure by his side.

'Sammy!' Fin knelt down and held out his arms. 'Where have you been?'

To his surprise, Sam turned away and held on to Mr Aldridge's leg. Buster sniffed round them for a moment, then scampered off among the bushes. Mr Aldridge smiled.

'Glad there's someone in. I was worried you might all be out looking for him.'

'Where was he?' said Fin.

'Just down from the coastal path.'

Fin looked at Sam again but Sam spoke first. 'Leave me alone.'

'What's up, Sammy?'

'Leave me alone.'

Mr Aldridge shook his head. 'I couldn't believe it when I saw him there all on his own.'

'I wasn't on my own,' said Sam.

'Mr Aldridge thinks you were,' said Fin.

'I wasn't.'

'So who was with you?'

'It's a secret.'

'OK, Sammy. But why were you out there?'

'It's a secret.'

'Is it a game?'

Sam said nothing. Fin tried to think. He must have just missed Sam when he was out that way himself, unless . . .

'Sammy? Did you pass me coming back from the cliffs?'

Sam didn't answer.

'Did you, Sammy? Please tell me.'

Sam bit his lip, then nodded.

'So why didn't I see you?' said Fin.

'I was hiding.'

'Hiding from me?'

'Yes.'

'Where?'

'It's a secret.'

'Oh, come on, Sammy.'

Sam was silent for a while, then he said: 'I hid at the side of the track. You didn't see me 'cause it was dark. I hid when I saw Mr Aldridge, too, and he didn't see me, but Buster came up and sniffed me and then Mr Aldridge saw me.'

'But what did you hide for?'

'She told me to. She told me you'd make me come home if you saw me.'

'Who, Sammy?'

But Sam was silent again. Fin straightened up and tried to think of a tactful way to get rid of Mr Aldridge, but at that moment Mum burst through the gate.

'Sam!' she said. She rushed over and picked him up.

'Mr Aldridge brought him home,' said Fin.

Mum seemed not to hear. She was stroking Sam's head and kissing him. 'My love,' she said. 'We've been so worried about you. Where have you been?'

There was no time for Sam to answer. Dad had also appeared at the gate. Mum saw him and called over. 'He's fine, Peter. Nothing to worry about. I've told him you're not angry with him.'

'You've—?' Dad stopped, seeing Mr Aldridge standing there. Mr Aldridge nodded to him, then looked round at Mum.

'I'll be on my way. Glad nothing's amiss.'

'Thanks so much for bringing him back,' said Mum.

'No problem.'

Dad walked up, all smiles now, and shook hands with Mr Aldridge. 'Do we have you to thank for this?'

'No thanks needed. I'm glad to have been of help.'

'Well, it's very kind of you. Sam's been a little highly strung lately.'

'Ah, well. No harm done. Ella's all right, is she?'

'Fine. She's in London at the moment.'

'Oh, that explains it.'

'Explains what?'

'Explains why I didn't see her out on Biscuit this morning. There aren't many days when I don't see her and Angie riding past my house.' He whistled for Buster. 'Come on, boy.'

'Well, we're really grateful for your help,' said Dad. 'I'd ask you in for a cup of tea but I think we'd better get this little chap to bed.'

'That's all right. Can't stop anyway. Back's giving me a bad time again and I've got to keep moving, like I told Fin.'

'Some other time,' said Dad.

'Yes.' Mr Aldridge gave him a quizzical smile. 'Some other time. Goodnight.' He headed for the gate, Buster at his heels, and soon disappeared down the lane. Dad looked at Sam, who had buried his face in Mum's neck.

'Where was he?' he said.

'On his way to the coastal path,' said Fin.

Mum took Sam up to bed; Dad went straight to the sitting room and closed the door behind him. Fin stood in the hall, listening, and a moment later heard the sound of his father pacing the floor. He hesitated, then pushed open the door and walked in. Dad made no attempt to disguise his irritation at being disturbed. He watched Fin for a moment, then threw himself in the armchair by the piano and stared at the wall.

'Dad?' said Fin.

'What do you want?'

'Have you . . . have you seen anyone strange or anything?'

'What do you mean?'

'Anyone hanging round the house?'

Dad's eyes narrowed. 'What have you seen?'

'I don't know, I just . . . ' He swallowed. 'I went up to the village square and saw this tramp hitchhiking. I don't know who he was. I just wondered if you'd seen him or anything.'

'No.' Dad looked sharply away. It was clear that the conversation was over; what was not clear was why Dad was lying. For a moment Fin thought of telling his father what he'd seen, but he knew he could not. There was something dangerously unpredictable—even frightening—about Dad right now.

He walked back to the door, stopped and turned. Dad was watching him, his face impassive, and the silence between them felt like a wall. Fin left the room, closed the door behind him and leaned against it, trying to think; but it was hard to think. All he wanted to do was shriek, just as he had shrieked earlier, and this time he wanted Mum and Dad and Sam and all the world to hear it; especially Ella. More than anyone else, he wanted Ella to hear it.

He walked to the foot of the stairs and saw Mum coming down. She stopped and put her arms round him and held him. 'Be strong, Fin,' she whispered. 'I need you to be strong.' Her hand was soft on his hair and she was stroking him. He knew she was crying, though she made no sound. He stretched his arms round her back and pulled her closer, and they held each other, neither speaking; then she drew back and kissed him on the cheek.

'Thank you, darling.'

She stood there a moment longer, still stroking his hair, her eyes on his; then suddenly she turned away, walked off to the kitchen and closed the door behind her. He made his way up the stairs and wandered down the landing towards his room, but the sound of Sam's voice made him stop. He crept forward. The door to Sam's room was ajar and there was a glow inside. Mum must have left the corner lamp on so that Sam wouldn't be frightened. He took a step closer and listened.

There was the voice again, that strange, dream-like voice, but it was hard to hear the words. He peeped round the door. Sam didn't see him. He was tucked up in bed with Teddy and staring towards his secret cupboard. There was no one else in the room. He was murmuring to an empty space.

'I can't come. I can't come. I can't come.'

10

Ella was running, running for her life. The coastal path twisted before her and she tore along it into the storm. She saw clouds racing, bracken flailing, sea smashing on the rocks; she saw the Pengrig lighthouse rising like a sword. She raced towards it, the wind driving her on, and still the terror pursued her, the huge unseen presence she sensed behind her, chasing, chasing. She could hear it panting after her. She could feel its hands reaching out to clutch her. The cliff-edge rushed closer and the jaws of the sea opened beneath her, foaming. She cried out and woke to see a huge form leaning over her in the darkness.

'No!' she screamed. 'No! No! No!'

The boy's hand was stretching towards her hair again but it froze, then slowly moved back. He stared down at her, his face darker than the night. She watched, gulping for breath and listening even now for the sounds of the storm that had haunted the nightmare. But they were gone; the chamber was still. The boy straightened up.

'Dreaming,' he said. His voice sounded flat, as though he wanted to squeeze all emotion from it. 'You're dreaming.' He watched her in silence for a moment, then looked away. 'I know about dreaming.'

'It wasn't a dream,' she said. 'It was a nightmare.'

'I know.' He looked back at her, then—with a brusqueness that startled her—turned away, strode to the far side of the chamber and lay down on his back. She tried to stop shaking but it was no good: this boy terrified her no matter what he did. He'd seemed almost calm a moment ago and all he was doing now was staring up at the ceiling, but the anger she'd seen in him before was still close to the surface; she sensed it boiling inside him. She watched him for several minutes, then, keeping her eyes firmly upon him, eased herself down onto her side. The silence deepened around them, broken only by their breathing and the soft percussion of the sea.

He moved suddenly, just a glance towards her, then, with the same brusqueness as before, rolled onto his side so that his back was towards her. She watched, still trembling. What had she done and what did he want? Part of him yearned to touch her hair, part of him to have nothing to do with her; and part of him ached to kill her. She knew it, she felt it, she saw it in his face.

She kept her eyes upon him, shivering more and more as the night chill crept over her from the tunnel and the gaps in the rockface. Yet in a strange way she was glad of this; she wanted no sleep tonight, not while he was here, and the cool air would help keep her awake. The pictures from the nightmare slipped back into her mind.

'Go away,' she muttered. 'Go away, go away.'

But they clung to her like a bad smell. She thought of Mum and Dad and Fin and Sam; then just Sam. Little Sam. Tears filled her eyes.

'Sammy,' she said softly, 'Sammy.'

The pictures of the nightmare still bulged in her mind.

'Little Sammy, little Sammy.'

They stayed a few moments longer, then flickered and vanished. She stared into the night and looked for Sam's face but all she saw was the empty blackness of the chamber. Then the image came: the tiny face, the soft hair, the bright eyes.

'Sammy,' she murmured. 'Little Sammy.'

The face peered through the darkness at her.

'Are you sleeping, Sammy? Are you sleeping?'

She felt her eyes close in spite of her fear.

'You're sleeping,' she whispered. 'I know you are.'

But Sam was not sleeping. He was sitting up in bed. The little girl in the pretty white dress was standing there again, speaking to him in that musical voice he liked so much yet found so strange. Strange because it didn't sound like a normal voice. It seemed to come from inside his own head, just like when he listened to his other secret friends.

She smiled.

He liked that, too. She was always smiling and she had golden hair just like Ella. She even looked like Ella, though she could only be about three years old, the same as him. She was so beautiful. He tried the usual question.

'What's your name?' he said aloud.

And the usual answer came back inside his head.

Come and play.

'I won't tell anyone.'

Come and play.

And she beckoned him towards the door.

He hesitated. He wanted to go with her again. He loved being with her. She was so like Ella. But Mummy had told him he mustn't run away again.

Come and play.

'I can't come. I promised Mummy I won't run away.'

We're not going to run away. We're just going to play.

And he climbed out of bed, leaving Teddy behind, and followed her out of the door. The landing was dark but the gold of the little girl's hair seemed to glow like the sun. The door to Fin's room was closed and no sound came from within but from Mummy and Daddy's room he heard muttering. It sounded like Daddy. The little girl turned and put a finger to her lips.

Can you see the monsters sleeping?

He stared at the dark shapes all around and nodded. She looked at him.

We must be quiet or we'll wake them.

'OK.'

Sssh!

And they crept on, past Mummy and Daddy's room and down the stairs to the hall. The little girl turned and looked at him again.

Let's play in the garden.

'I mustn't. I promised Mummy I won't run away.'

We're not going to run away. We're just going to play in the garden.

And she started to walk down the hall towards the back door. He followed, reluctant to leave her. She stopped in the kitchen and turned. He walked up to her. He wished she'd let him touch her. He always

100

touched Ella and Fin when he played with them but the little girl never let him get too close. But he was close enough now. He stretched out a hand. She drew back, just out of reach, and smiled again.

Open the back door.

He looked up at it. It didn't seem right. The little girl's voice spoke again inside his head.

Go on. Just like you did last time.

He reached up, twisted the handle and pulled the door towards him. It would not move.

The bolt, said the little girl.

He fumbled with the bolt. It seemed to make an awful noise but eventually it slid across. He turned the handle and this time pulled the door open. Cool air brushed his skin. The little girl ran out into the garden, her hair tumbling about her face. He left the door open and sped after her across the lawn. It was damp and it felt exciting to be running barefoot over the grass. She was already far ahead of him and racing down towards the stable. He hurried after her but couldn't keep up. She was such a fast runner. She reached the stable and disappeared round the side.

He ran on and stopped by the entrance. There was no sign of her. He looked around him, suddenly frightened. The sky was dark and there were big clouds like faces. The moon had appeared behind one of them and it looked cold and scary. He wished he'd brought Teddy with him.

You can't see me, said the voice in his head.

'Yes, I can!' he called.

No, you can't.

'I can!'

So where am I?

But it was no good. He couldn't see her. From

inside the stable came a sound of hooves scratching at the ground. He looked about him, close to tears. He wanted to run back to the house but in his confusion he wasn't sure which way to go. Everything seemed dark and frightening.

Look behind you, said the voice.

He whirled round. Somewhere over by the bushes a small shadow was moving. He started to run over. The shadow disappeared. He ran as far as the bushes and stopped. The voice spoke again.

You're warm. Look around you.

He looked to the left and saw only the wall that bordered the orchard.

I'm not there.

He looked to the right.

Not there either.

'Where are you?' he called.

Look behind you.

He turned and saw her running back up the slope towards the house. He ran after her, glad to see her again, but once more she was leaving him behind. She reached the house ahead of him and ran to the right, past the open back door, and round the side of the building.

He followed, still frightened but not as much as he had been a moment ago when he'd thought he was all alone. He reached the side of the building. There was no sign of the little girl. All he could see was the grass at the back of the house and the outline of the fence that cut their land from the fields beyond.

He ran on, tired now, but determined to catch up with her. He felt sure she would be behind the house. Unless she had run all the way round. He reached the far edge of the wall and stared about him.

No sign of her. He felt his lip tremble. The voice spoke to him playfully.

Come on. You still haven't found me.

'Where are you?' he called.

He wanted to see her so much. He didn't like this running and chasing. He wanted to sit down and talk to her and look at her. But she was making fun of him.

I'm not making fun of you.

'You are.'

I'm not.

'Where are you?'

Look to the left.

He stared through the darkness and saw her head peeping round the side of the house. A moment later it disappeared. He ran towards the end of the building, now desperate to catch her. He felt sure she was going to vanish again but he ran as fast as he could and tore round the side of the house.

To his surprise she was standing there, right in front of him. He stopped, panting for breath. He didn't want to show her he'd been frightened. She didn't seem frightened at all and she wasn't out of breath either. She smiled at him.

Let's play out in the lane.

'I can't. I promised Mummy.'

We're only going to play. Come on.

And she turned and ran towards the gate. Instinctively he followed. She didn't run fast this time and he knew she was letting him keep up with her. It felt good. She laughed as she ran, a loud gurgling chuckle that sounded good in his head, and he laughed too. They reached the gate and she stopped and looked round at him.

You go first.

He hesitated. He'd promised Mummy faithfully but the little girl was being so friendly, and they were only going to play. He wouldn't run away or anything. They'd just play for a while, then he'd go home and curl up with Teddy and sleep. He pushed open the gate and walked into the lane. The little girl skipped past him, then stopped and pulled a face. It was so funny. He pulled a face back and she giggled. He ran up to her and reached out to tug her hair, but she squirmed away, giggling again, and his hand caught nothing but air.

She ran on up the lane. He followed, uneasy to be moving away from the house towards the cliffs but glad not to be alone. The wind was growing stronger but he didn't mind because the little girl wasn't hiding from him any more. She stopped at the forked track and waited for him to catch up.

Let's go to the coastal path and play.

'I mustn't,' he said. 'I mustn't.'

This time he knew he mustn't go any further. The little girl smiled.

There's a storm coming. Can you feel it?

'No.'

It's coming. It's coming very soon. Let's go and catch it.

'You can't catch a storm.'

You can. If you jump up into the sky. But you've got to be careful.

'What for?'

You've got to catch the storm before the storm catches you.

And without waiting for him to answer she ran on up the track towards the coastal path. He stood there, already starting to feel frightened as she faded from view in the darkness. He took a deep breath and raced after her.

Fin sat up in bed with a start. He was sure he'd heard something; a click of some kind. He listened for several minutes, then, hearing nothing, lay back again, confused. He'd been trying to sleep but had only been dozing fitfully, crazed with a dream of the kidnapper's voice. He could hear it so clearly, with all its cockiness and insolence, and he was starting to picture the face that went with it, but it kept changing. One moment it was this, the next it was that. It seemed to mock him, just as the voice did. Probably the click was part of the dream, too.

He lay there for some time, gazing up at the ceiling and thinking of Ella, then restlessness seized him once more and he jumped out of bed and wandered over to the window. The night sky had changed. It was pale now. The clouds were moving and the moon was throwing a ghostly light over the garden. He tensed suddenly.

The gate was open.

He was sure Mr Aldridge had shut it behind him when he left. Maybe there really had been a click and it was the sound of someone coming in. He thought of the kidnapper and the drunken tramp and ran his eyes over the bushes and lawn. There was no sign of anyone but he knew that meant nothing. An intruder could have slipped round the other side of the house and be breaking in right this moment.

He walked through to the landing and stopped outside Mum and Dad's room. The door was ajar and he peeped through the gap, expecting to see them both wide awake, but to his surprise they were asleep, though they were lying on top of the duvet and neither had changed out of their day clothes. Dad was twitching as he slept but Mum looked somehow child-like, and he quickly understood why.

She had pulled her knees into her chest and was lying there, curled up in a ball. For a moment he almost felt he was looking at Sam. She had turned her back to Dad and he to her, and they seemed much further apart than the few inches that separated them. Fin watched, glad they were sleeping, especially Mum. He had thought she would never sleep again while this was going on.

It was pointless waking them when he wasn't even sure about the click and, besides, there could easily be a simple explanation for the open gate. Mrs Wilder might have dropped by to push the parish magazine through the letterbox. She often delivered it late at night. He closed the door on Mum and Dad and made his way towards the stairs to check, but the sight of Sam's door stopped him.

It was wide open and the room was empty. Only Teddy lay in the bed, his head just visible above the sheet. Fin searched the cupboard to make sure, but there was no sign of Sam. He crept downstairs. The little boy couldn't have gone far. He'd never leave Teddy behind if he was going any distance and surely he'd be too tired, too upset, and too frightened of Mum and Dad being angry to run away again. But the open back door told another story.

'Oh, no,' Fin murmured. 'Not again.'

He hurried to his room and dressed, glad there were no sounds of movement from Mum and Dad's room. He knew he should wake them; but he also knew he wasn't going to. Sam would be in big trouble this time if they found out and, anyway, it was obvious where the little boy had gone, though for what reason he could not guess.

He picked up his torch, stole out of the back door to the lane and raced towards the cliffs, flashing the beam ahead of him. Sam had hidden last time and would probably do so again. But the torch picked up nothing. He reached the fork at the end of the lane and ran down the track towards the coastal path.

Still no sign of anyone. The land dipped before him and he saw the sea stretching away, speckled with moonlight. He slowed down, scanning the snarls of bracken with the torch. He had found Sam here before but this time he saw nothing. He walked down to the cliff-edge and stopped at the signpost by the coastal path.

Maybe Sam hadn't come this far. If he had, there were only two ways to go: left to the cove or right to Pengrig. The third hideous possibility was too frightening to contemplate. He turned to the right and ran towards Pengrig. The coastal path seemed as deserted now as it had been earlier but he ran on until the shadowy form of the old lighthouse broke into view. And there, scampering towards it, was a tiny figure.

It had to be Sam. Fin switched off the torch and raced after him. The distance quickly closed between them and he soon saw he was right. It was Sam and he was running blindly towards the cliff-edge, apparently unaware that he was being followed. As Fin drew closer, he heard him calling.

'Wait! Wait!'

But it was not to him. It was to someone else,

someone Fin couldn't see. Fin made to call out himself, then changed his mind. With the cliff-edge so close, it could be dangerous to startle Sam. He ran on, caught Sam round the waist and lifted him off his feet. Sam screamed at once, wriggling and writhing in Fin's arms.

'Sammy, it's me! It's only me!'

'Let me go!'

'It's all right. Everything's all right.'

'Let me go!'

'Sssh.' Fin hugged Sam to him. 'It's all right, Sammy. Don't be frightened.'

Sam started sobbing, his eyes straining towards the lighthouse, then suddenly, as though a spell had been broken, they closed and he buried his face in Fin's chest. Fin talked on as softly as he could and gradually the body relaxed in his arms, but he stood there for several minutes, rocking Sam as the beam from the automatic lighthouse flashed over them. Then he kissed Sam on the head.

'All right now, Sammy?'

'There's a storm coming.'

'No, there isn't. It's a lovely night. Nice and settled. Nothing to worry about.'

'There is. It's coming. She said so.'

'Who?'

Sam didn't answer. Fin kissed him again.

'Well, if there is a storm coming, it won't be anything to be frightened of.'

'Going to catch it,' said Sam.

'Catch it? Catch what?'

'The storm. Going to catch the storm.'

'You can't catch a storm, Sammy.'

'You can. If you jump up into the sky.'

Fin frowned. This was getting more disturbing by the minute. He thought of Sam's wild run towards the cliff and shuddered. 'Sammy, there isn't going to be a storm, OK? There's nothing to worry about.'

'I want to go home.'

'OK, Sammy.'

He didn't bother taking Sam by the hand and walking. He carried him. Sam clung to him, whimpering, and Fin decided not to speak. By the time they had reached Polvellan Sam was asleep in his arms. He looked over the house. There were no lights on and no sign that Mum or Dad had woken up. With any luck he'd be able to get Sam back into bed without them knowing anything of this, at least for now. He glanced down.

The moonlight on Sam's face made him look otherworldly and for a moment Fin almost felt he was holding a tiny angel. He carried him in through the back door, locked it behind them, then, still carrying Sam, crept through the hall and up the stairs. There was no sound from Mum and Dad. He entered Sam's room, tucked him up in bed and moved Teddy closer. When he straightened up, he found he was shaking.

There was nothing more to be done for the moment. He would see how Sam was in the morning before deciding whether to mention this to Mum and Dad. He returned to his room, changed back into his pyjamas, and climbed into bed; then climbed straight out again.

It was no good. He knew he wouldn't settle. He went back to Sam's room, drew a chair up to the bed and slumped in it. Sam had curled into a ball, just as Mum had done earlier, but he seemed contented enough now. Fin yawned and leaned back in the chair, thinking of Ella, and Mum and Dad, and Sam's strange behaviour, and wondering what the new day would bring.

11

The new day brought the voice. The phone rang at eight o'clock in the morning. Mum picked Sam up without a word and took him into the hall; Dad glanced at Fin and pressed the speaker button on the phone. 'Yes?'

'Good morning, Mr Parnell,' sneered the voice. 'And how are we today?'

'I want to speak to Ella.'

'Have you arranged the money like a good boy?'

'I'll be collecting it this morning. I want to speak to Ella.'

'Well, you can't.'

'So how do I know she's alive?'

'You don't.' The voice gave an elaborate sigh. 'We've been through this and I'm getting bored. The conditions are simple. You pay the money and you see her. You don't and she's dead. End of story. Or rather, end of your daughter.'

'It's perfectly reasonable my wanting to speak to her. Haven't you got any feelings?'

'Not where you're concerned. Get the money by lunchtime. I'll ring you then.'

'But—'

There was a click and the phone went dead.

Mum appeared in the doorway, still carrying Sam. He had thrown his arms round her neck and was clinging to her, snuffling. He seemed locked within himself and had been crying on and off since dawn. Fin watched, fighting exhaustion from his own lack of sleep and wondering whether to say anything about last night. So far Mum and Dad knew nothing. He'd managed to slip back to bed just before they woke up, then Sam had started bawling and taken all their attention.

He decided to keep silent. There seemed little to be gained by talking about it now. Mum looked down at Sam, then lowered her voice. 'Peter, was that . . . ?'

'Yes,' said Dad. 'Fin and I'll go into Newquay. You'd better stay here with Sam.'

Fin walked up and looked Sam over. The boy's eyes were tightly closed as though he wanted to block out the world. 'Mum,' he said, 'is he going to be all right?'

'He's quietening down now.' She kissed Sam. 'Aren't you, sweetheart?'

Sam's eyes opened for a few seconds but he said nothing. Mum looked round at Fin, then leaned across and kissed him, too. 'Good luck, darling. Take care.'

'OK.'

'Peter?' She looked at Dad. 'Take care.'

'I will.' He stared at her for a moment and she at him, both motionless, both tight-lipped; then he turned and picked up the car keys.

'Right, Fin. Let's go.'

They didn't speak much in the car and Fin wasn't sure which of them was more tense. He felt edgy enough himself and he desperately needed sleep but Dad looked ready to snap at the slightest provocation. They reached the outskirts of Newquay and headed for the town centre. Parnell's Superstore appeared on the right but Dad didn't spare it a glance. His eyes were fixed on the road, his foot hard down on the accelerator, as though he couldn't reach the bank quickly enough.

Two minutes later they were stuck in a traffic jam. Dad craned his head out of the window and peered forward. 'God, if it's like this in town, we'll never get a parking spot near the bank.'

When they finally reached the town centre, they found the streets swarming with jaywalkers, some carrying surfboards to the beach, others wandering across to the chip shops and amusement arcades.

'Keep your eyes peeled for somewhere to park,' said Dad.

But every spot seemed to be taken. They drove round in vain for half an hour, Dad growing increasingly impatient. Finally he pulled in to the car park by the bowling club.

'It's full,' said Fin.

Dad ignored him and drove to the yellow hatching by the telephone boxes.

'We're not supposed to park here,' said Fin.

'I know that but I can't be fiddling round here for ever. We've got to get back by midday. If that bastard phones and we're not there, we could be sunk.' He backed the car into the hatching and switched off the engine. 'Now listen, you're to stay here. I don't want you leaving the car under any circumstances. If an attendant turns up, just say we've got an emergency.'

'What kind of emergency?'

'Christ, I don't know. Just say whatever comes into your head. Say your little brother's got lost and your dad's rushed off to find him or something.'

Fin thought of last night but said nothing. Dad handed over the car keys and some coins. 'Get a ticket from the machine. It might help. If anyone asks, say I'll be back any second.'

'OK.'

'See you later.' And Dad was gone. Fin watched him disappear in the crowd, then gave a start. Shambling down from the other end of the street was an unmistakable figure.

It was the tramp. He watched the man through narrowed eyes. The lurch in the step was more pronounced than ever and he was clearly drunk. Two boys with skateboards ran up the street; the man stopped them and spoke. They shook their heads and ran past him. He sloped over to an elderly lady walking a spaniel; she, too, shook her head, and the man continued down the street.

He was begging.

Fin watched, unsure what to do. He knew he shouldn't leave the car but he might not have another chance to find out more about this tramp. He bought a ticket from the machine and stuck it on the inside of the windscreen, then locked the doors and raced over to the street. The man had disappeared from view but he couldn't have gone far. Fin ran down the road and soon spotted him heading down Harbour Hill.

He followed for a few yards and stopped by the railings at the top of the rise. The sea below was bathed in stillness but the harbour was fussy with activity. Many of the fishing boats had crews aboard, the little beach was crowded with swimmers, and there were queues at the huts for boat trips. The tramp reached the bottom of the hill and slouched over to the café. Fin's eyes never left him. He waited for a few moments, then made his way down to the harbour.

The man seemed unaware of him. His attention was on whoever was nearest and it didn't seem to matter who that was. He spoke to everyone, presumably asking each person for money. No one gave him any. Fin drew closer and stopped. The tramp seemed to have given up with the café and was shuffling towards the lifeboat station. Fin stepped into his path.

The tramp stopped and fixed him with a stare. 'Spare me a cup of tea, mate?'

The voice was hoarse, the words slurred. Fin felt in his pocket. He had a few coins left from the ones Dad had given him. He pulled them out, aware of the man swaying close by, and tried to think of some way of coaxing him to talk.

'Where do you live?' he said after a moment. 'Round here?'

The man licked his lips, his eyes on the coins in Fin's hand. He clearly didn't want to talk. He just wanted to take the money and move on to the next person. Fin pretended to sort through the coins. The tramp's eyes flicked up at him.

'I don't live nowhere special,' he said eventually.

Fin studied the face. It was weather-beaten and craggy and the eyes were tired and glazed. There were no signs of recognition. Yet this man knew Dad.

He handed over the coins, unable to think of

anything else to say. The man took them without a word and shuffled on. Fin watched him for a moment, then heard a voice behind him. 'Not a good idea.'

He turned and saw a policeman standing there.

'What's not a good idea?'

'Giving money to beggars,' said the policeman. 'Specially wasters like Kelman.'

'Kelman?'

'Francis Kelman.' The policeman glanced towards the tramp, who had just stopped a group of boys outside the rowing club. 'He's not too bad when he's sober but when he's had a few, he can turn nasty. He'll spend your contribution on booze. You're not doing him any favours giving him money.'

Fin looked away. He knew he ought to get back but he was still desperate to find some connection between this tramp and Dad. He looked at the policeman again.

'Where does he live? I haven't seen him around.'

'Dosses all over the place—Newquay, St Ives, Penzance, Padstow. Seems to like places round the coast. I saw a lot of him when I was a junior policeman, then about ten years ago he disappeared and we thought we'd got rid of him. God knows where he went but he turned up again a few weeks ago like a bad penny.' The policeman flexed his muscles. 'Which is a shame. We could do without the likes of him round here.'

And he lumbered over to the tramp to move him on. Fin didn't wait to see more; he'd learned all he could. He turned and ran back up the hill, more confused than ever about this man and now anxious about the car.

116

But all was well; and here was Dad hurrying towards him.

Mum was waiting nervously in the hall.

'What's happened?' said Dad. 'Where's Sam?'

'It's all right,' she said. 'He's in the sitting room.'

'Has he stopped crying?'

'Yes. But . . . ' She looked down.

'What's happened?'

'That boy phoned. The one from the kidnappers. Where have you been? Why weren't you here?'

'It was the traffic. We got held up.' Dad grabbed her by the arm. 'What did he say?'

'He said you'd better be here next time he phones or we can forget about seeing Ella again.'

Dad clenched his fists. 'If that boy's done something to Ella, I'll kill him.' The telephone rang. Dad strode over and pressed the speaker button. 'Yes?' he snapped.

'You're late.' It was the voice, goading. 'I want to speak to the boy with the blue jacket.'

'Well, you can speak to me.'

'I don't want to speak to you. I want to speak to the boy with the blue jacket.'

'Well, you can't. It's me or nobody.'

'Then it's nobody. Bye.'

And the phone went dead.

'Peter!' Mum seized him by the shoulder. 'You stupid man! You stupid, stupid man!'

'Mummy?' called a voice.

Fin whirled round and saw Sam standing in the doorway. Mum rushed over and picked him up. 'It's all right, my love. It's all right.'

'What are you crying for?'

'I'm not crying. It's all right.' She kissed him. 'Mummy's just upset about something but everything's all right now.'

Dad looked away. 'I didn't mean . . . I . . . '

The phone rang again. Fin saw Mum and Dad turn towards him. Neither spoke but he did not need them to. He walked forward and pressed the speaker button. 'Yes?'

'Now that's more like it,' jeered the voice. Fin took a deep breath, fighting the urge to shriek down the phone. Mum gave his arm a squeeze, then took Sam by the hand, hurried with him out to the hall, and closed the door behind them.

'What do you want?' said Fin.

'I want you to do exactly what I say. If you don't, you'll only have yourself to blame for your sister's death.'

'What do you want me to do?'

'Have you got the money?'

'Yes.'

'Have you counted it?'

'My father has.'

'Have you got a nice big bag?'

'Yes.'

'What a clever boy.'

Fin took another deep breath, trying desperately to calm himself. Close by he saw Dad standing stiffly erect, his eyes staring fixedly at the phone. Mum returned, alone.

'You're to put all the money in the bag,' said the voice. 'It must be the full amount. If it's anything less, you can kiss goodbye to your sister. Well, you won't be able to kiss goodbye because she'll be dead, but you get the point.'

'It'll all be there.'

'Good boy. You're picking this up so quickly I feel we could almost be friends.'

'Get on with it, you shit!' Fin felt the words fly out of him before he could stop them. Mum and Dad shot agonized glances at him. There was a long silence, then the voice spoke again.

'Sorry, did I touch a nerve there?'

'What do you want me to do with the money?'

'Easy, easy,' said the voice. 'You're starting to sound like your father and we don't want that, do we?' Fin glanced at Dad and saw his face taut with fury. Mum moved closer, her eyes moving from one to the other. 'Now then,' said the voice, 'you'll need two mobile phones. Charged up.'

'Why two?'

'Never mind why two. Just do as you're told. You can borrow one from your father and one from your mother. I presume they've each got one. Or maybe you've got one of your own. I'm sure Daddy's bought you one.'

'My parents have both got one.'

'How nice for them. And your father's number is?'

'What?'

'Your father's number. Come on, I was just starting to think you had a brain. What's the bloody number?'

Dad scribbled the number on the pad by the phone and pushed it across. Fin read it out.

'That wasn't too painful, was it?' said the voice. 'Now listen. I don't want to have to repeat myself. You switch on both mobile phones, take the bag with the money, and walk out of the house. You take the lane towards the village and keep walking.'

Dad broke in. 'Now wait a minute—'

'Get back in your cage, Parnell.'

'I'm not having Fin take the money. I'll do it.'

'You're wasting my time. You and your wife'll stay at home if you want to see your daughter. Now, can I speak to the boy again or shall we call the whole thing off?'

'I'm here,' said Fin.

'Then pay attention. I'm getting impatient. You take the lane towards the village and wait till the phone rings. And don't try anything stupid. There's lots of us watching you. One slip up and it's the end of the girl.'

'It's OK. I'll do as you say.' Fin frowned. There was no point in arguing. The boy held all the cards. Dad scribbled a note and pushed it across. Fin glanced down and read it out. 'What about Ella? Where will we find her?'

'That's not your problem. You do your bit, then we'll let you know about the girl.'

'But how do we know you're going to give her back?'

'You don't. Tough, isn't it? Now get started.'

But before Fin could respond, another voice spoke: a strange, dreamy voice, a voice he knew yet hardly recognized.

'There's a storm coming. Going to catch it.'

He turned and saw Sam standing in the doorway again.

'Who the hell's that?' snapped the kidnapper. Sam's eyes widened like ripples in a lake. The kidnapper shouted: 'Who the hell's that?'

Fin gasped at the sudden change in the voice. In a matter of seconds the confidence had vanished; in

120

its place he heard confusion, anger, fear. Sam spoke again, his eyes staring upwards.

'Going to jump up into the sky and catch the storm before it catches me.' And he ran off down the hall towards the front door, Mum hurrying after him. The kidnapper bawled down the phone.

'I said who the hell's that?'

'My little brother,' said Fin.

'Well, tell him to shut up!'

Fin said nothing.

'Tell him to shut up!' screamed the voice. 'Do you hear?'

'I hear you.'

'And get yourself out of the house!'

The phone went dead. Fin walked over to the doorway and stared down the hall. The front door was closed and Sam was sitting in front of it, fiddling with the mat. Mum was kneeling beside him. 'What is it, Sam?' she was saying. 'What's upsetting you?'

Sam looked away and said nothing. Fin felt a tap on the shoulder and turned to see Dad standing there with the two mobile phones. 'Here.' Dad held them out. 'I don't know why they need two but we'd better follow instructions. They're obviously going to talk you through whatever they want you to do. With my one you press this button when it rings. With your mum's—'

'I know how they work.'

'OK.' Dad handed them over and lowered his voice. 'Listen, don't argue with them. Just do what they say—within reason. Don't put yourself at risk. I could maybe try and follow. If I keep well back, I could—'

'Dad, forget it.' Fin glanced at Sam and lowered

his voice, too. 'It only wants one of them to see you and we could lose Ella.' He thought for a moment. 'That boy sounded really scared when Sammy piped up. What do you think it means?'

'I don't know.' Dad looked him over. 'Go on. You'd better get out there. But keep your wits about you, OK? And for Christ's sake, be careful.'

'I will.'

He saw Mum hurrying towards him. 'Fin, darling.' She pulled him to her. 'Please . . . '

'I'll be OK.'

'Please, darling . . . just . . . '

'I'll be OK, Mum.'

She held him close. 'No silly risks, OK?'

'I promise.'

'Don't try and fight them or anything.'

'I won't. Please, Mum, I've got to go. I've got to do it now.'

She kissed him and stepped back but her eyes never left him for a moment. He reached out and gave her arm a squeeze, then picked up the bag with the money and headed for the front door. Sam was still fiddling with the mat. Fin bent down to him. 'Give me five, Sammy. I need it.' Sam looked up at him and they clapped palms together. Fin kissed him. 'Thanks, mate. Look after Mummy and Daddy.'

And without glancing back, he left the house and set off down the lane.

12

Dad's mobile soon rang. Fin pressed the button and put the phone to his ear. 'Yes?'

'Now do exactly what I say.' The voice was calm again, back in control, but something had changed. It was crisper, harder, more resolute than before. 'Walk down the hill as if you're going to the village.'

'I'm already doing that.'

'Never mind the yak. Just do as you're told. Keep the mobile switched on and close to your ear. If you miss an instruction, it'll be your fault. When you get to the bottom of the hill, climb over the stile into the field and wait there.'

So that was the plan. Make it look as though he were going to the village, then send him somewhere else. He walked down the lane, Dad's phone tight to his ear. The voice was silent at the other end of the line but he sensed the boy was still there. Before long he saw the stile to the footpath just opposite the entrance to Billy's house.

He glanced to the right, hoping no one would see him—he could do without interference from the Meades right now—but the house and garden seemed deserted. He climbed over the stile and waited for the voice to speak. No words came. He looked around him, searching for signs that he was being watched.

There were none—yet the kidnapper could not be far away. Perhaps he was using the payphone in the village square. For a crazy moment Fin thought of racing up there but he knew that would be stupid. He could ruin everything by doing that. Besides, the boy might well be ringing from somewhere else and have accomplices hidden around the village. He wished the voice would speak again but still it was silent. He waited another minute, his hand twitching round the phone, then, unable to resist any longer, spoke into the mouthpiece.

'I'm here. What do I do now?'

'I know you're there,' said the voice. 'I can see you.'

'So why didn't you say something instead of leaving me standing here?'

'I'm playing with you. Making you sweat.'

Fin felt his muscles tighten. He looked around him again, trying to catch sight of someone watching. Perhaps the boy was using binoculars. He searched for a glint of sunlight on glass but in vain. The voice spoke again.

'Now this is where you have to be careful. If you don't do what I say, your sister'll pay for it. There are lots of us watching you so don't even think of trying anything on.'

'What do you want me to do?'

'Take the other phone and leave it on the ground by the stile. Put it by the left post as you're facing it.'

Fin took Mum's phone from his pocket and placed it on the ground.

'I've done that.'

'Now listen again. You're going to walk up the

field as far as the top, climb over the gate into the next field, walk to the top of that, then you're going to cut across to the track and make your way to the coastal path. You're not going to go up the lane or anywhere near your house—understand? You cut across the fields.'

'OK.'

'When you get to the coastal path, you're to walk down to the Pengrig lighthouse and wait by the fence.'

'Then what?'

'You wait for instructions. You can hang up this call now but leave the mobile switched on. And don't try ringing anybody. If we see anyone tracking you or turning up at the Pengrig, the girl's dead. Any questions?'

'No.'

'Clever boy. Now hang up the phone and get going.'

He hung up the call and started up the field, his stomach churning. He had no idea whether or not he was being watched. It was certainly possible. It would be easy enough to spy on him from a distance through binoculars and there were plenty of walls and fences to hide behind. Maybe there really were lots of people watching him or maybe it was just bluff. Presumably the boy—or someone else—was going to use Mum's phone to ring him but there was no point in hanging around the stile to find out. He had to obey the instructions to the letter. Ella's life was at stake.

He crossed both fields and climbed over the wall onto the track. The afternoon sun was hot but he started to feel the breeze as he drew closer to the sea. His head was groggy now from lack of sleep and he was starting to feel more and more vulnerable with all this money. He reached the brow of the land and stopped.

Below him was the carpet of bracken stretching down to the coastal path and beyond that the cliff, plunging into the sea. He made his way down to the path and turned in the direction of the Pengrig lighthouse. Once again he found his eyes searching for signs that he was being watched. The bracken was certainly thick enough to conceal someone but, as before, he saw no one.

He walked on, faster, faster. The path straightened out and he saw the automatic lighthouse ahead and, just beyond, the familiar form of the Pengrig, jutting against the sky. He was almost running now. He couldn't bear this waiting any longer. He fingered Dad's mobile, desperate for it to ring again, desperate even to hear the voice of the boy he despised, the boy he sensed close by, watching him, moving him, pulling his strings like a puppet master. He reached the Pengrig at last and stopped by the fence. The phone rang at once.

He pressed the button and put the phone to his ear. 'Now what?' he said.

'Wait for those people to go past.'

He looked round and saw an old man hobbling towards him on the arm of a woman about Mum's age. They were walking from the opposite direction and the man was clearly in some pain. Fin watched and waited, still listening into the phone. The voice spoke again.

'Drop your hand to the side. You look stupid standing there with that thing clapped to your ear. When they've gone past, you can put it back.'

Fin let his hand fall to the side. His eyes were racing now as he tried to work out where the boy was but there were so many hiding places: the bracken, the tower of the Pengrig, the automatic lighthouse up the slope. Wherever the boy was, he was keeping well out of sight. The man and the woman reached the fence and stopped, the old man leaning against her and breathing hard. He nodded to Fin.

'Nice afternoon.'

'Yes,' said Fin, wishing they would move on. The man gave a wheezy cough and glanced up at the Pengrig lighthouse.

'Can't see this old bugger lasting much longer.'

'No.'

'Be quite a sight when it goes, though. Wouldn't mind being around to see that. If I don't go first.' He gave another cough and winked at Fin. 'And I didn't mean over the edge.'

'Oh.'

The old man smiled and glanced at the woman, who rolled her eyes. 'Come on, Dad,' she said, and the two continued down the path. Fin watched them go, then put the phone back to his ear. There was a long silence, as though the boy were waiting for the two walkers to get well down the path; then the voice spoke again.

'Climb over the fence and take the bag into the Pengrig lighthouse.'

'What?'

'Take the bag into the Pengrig lighthouse!' shouted the kidnapper. 'Are you deaf or something?' Fin gave a start. Once more the voice had changed; the confidence had gone and fear was back, and with it, anger. The boy snapped at him. 'Do as you're told

127

and do it now before someone else comes along and we have to wait all over again.'

And suddenly, for the first time, Fin understood. This voice he'd been listening to—with all its brashness and mockery and swaggering scorn—was no more than an invention. It was not the real voice of the kidnapper at all but an act. This boy was as frightened as he was. Maybe more so.

'Hurry up,' said the voice.

He threw the bag over the fence, climbed up and dropped to the ground on the other side. He was quivering now with excitement and fear. He took the bag into the lighthouse and looked round. No one was there.

'Climb to the very top,' said the voice.

He started to climb. As with last time, the wind seemed louder from inside the building. He reached the lighthouse keeper's office and glanced quickly around him, waiting for an attack, but again there was no one here. He walked to the steps that led to the lantern and peered up. Ella had to be there; and the kidnappers. There was nowhere else they could be. He waited for a few moments, breathing hard, then started to climb.

But there was no one in the lantern. He spoke into the phone.

'What do I do now?'

'Take the bag out onto the balcony. If you've got the guts.'

He walked up to the opening. The broken door still hung loosely to the side and he made himself look through. Yesterday, in the darkness, the sight had been frightening enough. Now, in the terrifying clarity of daylight, it was worse. The lean of the tower took the lantern well over the edge of the cliff so that he felt suspended over the sea. The rocks below were white as the surf rolled in. He stepped out, holding the bag tightly to him, and felt the wind whirl round him. There was no one else here.

'Now what?' he shouted into the phone.

'Open the bag and look at the money.'

He opened the bag and stared at the neatly-bundled notes.

'Is it in little packs?' came the voice.

'Yes.'

'Of what? A hundred? A thousand?'

'I don't know. My dad counted them.'

'Take out one of the packs.'

He picked one up. The notes looked clean and stiff and somehow not like real money at all. He felt as though he were playing Monopoly.

'Break the seal round the pack,' said the voice.

He did as he was told.

'How does it feel?' said the voice.

'What?'

'How does the money feel? Come on, stupid. Play this game to the end.'

'It's not a game, you bastard!'

There was a silence and he felt a tremor of fear. He had tried so hard to hold back his feelings. He mustn't mess things up now. But the voice came back and this time it did not mock. 'You're right. It's not a game.'

There was another silence, a long one, as though each were waiting for the other to break it. It was Fin who did so. 'What do I do with the notes?'

'Throw them over the edge,' came the answer.

Fin stared at the money. A swirl of wind caught

his hair and flicked it into his eyes. 'Are you crazy?' he said.

It couldn't be this. The boy had to be joking. All this money. The voice spoke again. 'I'm not crazy. And you haven't thrown the money.'

Fin looked wildly about him and suddenly, at last, far down the coastal path, he caught a flash of sunlight; and with it a figure standing there, one arm raised to hold the phone, the other with binoculars—a huge, unforgettable figure, too far away for the features to be visible but close enough for him to know that this was his enemy.

'So now you see me,' said the voice. 'And I can see you. Now don't waste any more of my time. Throw the notes into the sea.'

'But . . . ' Fin looked down at them. 'You mean . . . just these ones . . . the ones I'm holding?'

'I mean all the notes, you stupid little shit.'

'But why? Why throw the money away? You must . . . you must want it.'

'There are some things worth more than money.'

'But if you don't want the money, then . . . what about Ella?'

'Do as I say or you can forget about Ella for ever.'

And Fin stretched back his arm and flung the notes over the edge. The wind caught them like confetti and scattered them seawards. He watched, his heart pounding, his eyes on the notes as they flew away.

'And the rest,' said the voice.

But he was already reaching into the bag. He broke the seals one by one and hurled the notes into the air. They fell like snowflakes into the mouths of foam. Again and again he reached down, again and again he threw out the notes; and when he was done, he picked up the bag and tipped it over the rail; and turned to look down the coastal path.

The figure was gone.

'Where's Ella?' he bellowed into the phone.

But the line was dead.

13

'You did what?' said Dad.

'I—'

'You threw the money away? You just . . . chucked it over the cliff?'

Fin stared back at him across the sitting room, unsure what to say. Mum stepped between them, her eyes on Dad. 'Don't you dare attack him. He's been really brave.'

'But—' Dad was still glaring at Fin. 'You climbed to the top of the Pengrig lighthouse and you just threw a hundred thousand pounds over the edge? Didn't it occur to you that if he was prepared to make you do that, then he never had the slightest intention of parting with Ella?'

Fin looked down. 'I didn't know what to think. I just felt, if I didn't do what he said, he might kill her.'

'He's probably done that already.'

'Peter!' Mum grabbed Dad by the arm. 'It's not Fin's fault. If you'd been carrying the money, you'd have had to do the same thing.'

'I'd at least have argued with the little bastard.'

'He's not little,' said Fin.

'What?' said Dad.

'He's not little. He's big, huge. Like a giant.'

'You saw him? Why the hell didn't you say so?'

'You didn't give me a chance.'

'Where were you when you saw him?'

'On the balcony of the Pengrig.'

'And where was he?'

'Down the coastal path.'

'On the Trevally side of the lighthouse?'

'No, the other side.'

'What did he look like?' said Mum.

'I couldn't see him clearly. He was too far away and he was holding binoculars up to his eyes, and I was a bit flustered being on the balcony and everything. All I really remember is how massive he was.'

A shadow seemed to pass over Dad's face but he said nothing. Mum spoke.

'The boy you saw can't have been the one we've been speaking to. He'd never have had time to get to the coastal path ahead of you. The nearest place he could have rung from is the payphone outside The Coppa Dolla, then he'd have had to run down, pick up my mobile from the stile and somehow get to the other side of the Pengrig before you turned up. It's just not possible.'

'It is,' said Fin. 'I worked it out. If he ran from the stile down the public footpath to the next fence, he could cut over to the cliffs across Roger Doyle's farm. He'd have had to run like mad but he could just about do it.'

'But where was he hiding when he was telling you to wait for those people to go past?'

'In the bracken probably.'

'Is it thick enough? I mean, if this boy's such a giant?'

Dad stirred. 'It's thick enough,' he said.

133

Fin looked round and saw the shadow cross his father's face again.

'Dad?' he said.

'What?'

'Have you got any enemies?'

''Course I have.' Dad shrugged. 'Anyone who's successful in business has enemies. It comes with the territory.'

'So who's behind all this?'

'How the hell do I know?' Dad scowled at him. 'Do you think I'd be standing here if I knew who it was? I want Ella back as much as you two.'

'Three,' said Mum. 'Don't forget Sam.'

'Two, three, whatever.' Dad turned to the window and stared out. Fin watched him for a moment, then looked back at Mum.

'Is Sammy any better?'

She shook her head. 'He's still very upset. He keeps crying and going on about a storm coming.'

'Where is he?'

'Up in his room.'

'Playing with Teddy?'

'Clinging to him more like. I'm really worried about him.' She looked at Dad, who was still staring out of the window. 'Peter, we must call the police in now.'

He turned round and faced her. 'That could make things worse.'

'But we can't just wait!'

'We've got to for a bit longer. The kidnapper might be just about to give her back. How do we know the money thing wasn't the whole point of this? Now that he's had his joke—'

'Joke? You call this a joke?'

'Well, perhaps not a joke but maybe a desire to hit out because we're rich. Call it what you like. He wants to make us suffer. Well, he's done that and we've kept our part of the bargain. He's never suggested that he wasn't going to give Ella back, as long as we did what he said, and now we have. I think we need to give him the chance to contact us again or let Ella go. If we bring the police in now and he gets wind of it, he could kill her.'

Mum walked up to him. 'I'll give it a few more hours but I'm not going to wait forever. If we haven't heard from that boy by the morning, I'm ringing the police whether you like it or not.'

There was a tense silence as Mum and Dad stared at each other. Then Fin spoke. 'Who's the tramp, Dad?'

Dad glanced at him. 'Tramp?'

'I asked you about him yesterday.'

'Is this important?'

'Who is he? What did he want?'

'Tramp?' said Mum. She looked at Dad. 'What's this about a tramp?'

'It's some guy Fin saw in the village.'

'And you know him,' said Fin.

'I don't know him.'

'I overheard you speaking to him in the lane. You told him not to come to the house any more.'

'Christ, is that all this is about?' Dad glowered at him. 'Haven't we got more important things to be talking about?' He turned to Mum. 'Some vagrant turned up at the house a few weeks ago asking for money. I gave him some coins and he cleared off. I thought nothing of it and forgot to even mention it. Then yesterday he turned up in the lane asking for some more. I told him to get lost.' He glared at Fin. 'Which is presumably what you heard.'

'So why did you say you hadn't seen him?'

'For God's sake, I've been that worried about Ella I can't even remember what I said five minutes ago, let alone yesterday. What is this—the Spanish Inquisition?'

'Stop it!' said Mum. 'Both of you. We mustn't fall out over this.' She looked from one to the other, then pulled Fin to her. 'Darling, have you not thought that you yourself might have some enemies?'

'Like who?'

'I don't know, but think. Is there anybody you've upset at school—anybody who might have a grudge against you? This boy's obviously about your age.'

'I can't think of anybody.'

'Well, chew it over. This thing could be related to you somehow.' She gave his arm a squeeze. 'I don't mean it's your fault, not for a moment. All I mean is, this boy maybe wants to get at you out of envy. He hasn't got what you've got and he wants to hit out at us by taking Ella. He certainly seems to have it in for you. Why would he insist on you carrying the money if it wasn't something personal?'

'Maybe he thought I'd be easier to handle than Dad. And if it's envy, why make me throw away the money? Why not keep it?' He looked away. This conversation was going nowhere and he felt so strung up now he wanted to scream. 'I'm going to my room,' he said. He started to pull away but felt Mum's hand tighten on his arm. 'I'm OK, Mum,' he said. 'Don't worry about me. I just need to be by myself.'

'Promise you won't go out of the house.'

'I promise.'

She gave him a hug. 'You were very brave today, Fin.'

'Thanks.'

'There was nothing else you could have done.'

'Oh, sure.'

'I mean it. There was nothing else you could have done.'

He said nothing. Mum kissed him. 'If you need us, we'll be down here by the phone.'

But Fin knew that was a waste of time. Somehow he understood that the boy would not ring again, that he had severed contact. Perhaps it was hearing that voice on the phone, hearing it lose control for those brief moments, that had opened a tiny window into the boy's mind. He had seen fear there, and desperate purpose. The business with the money had been more than just a taunt; it had been an act of pride. There was something else the kidnapper wanted, something far deeper. It had to be revenge—but what had they done, and who was it that hated them so much?

He walked upstairs, more anxious than ever about Ella, and wandered down to Sam's room. The door was ajar and he peeped round. Sam was curled up on the bed, facing the far wall, Teddy held close. Fin watched for a moment, listening for the sound of slow breathing that would tell him Sam was asleep; but he heard only restless gasps. He stepped into the room.

'Sammy?'

Sam stirred but didn't look at him. Fin knelt by the bed.

'Sammy, you OK?'

No answer. He stretched out a hand and stroked

137

the boy's head. Sam dug his nose into the pillow. Fin knew the signs and stood up to leave but, to his surprise, Sam spoke. 'There's a storm coming.'

'No, there isn't, Sammy.'

'Going to catch it. Going to catch the storm.'

'There's no storm coming, Sammy. It's a lovely day outside. Nothing to worry about.'

Sam said no more. Fin walked out to the landing and stopped by the window. The garden was bathed in sunlight and the conifers by the stable were barely moving in the breeze. There was no hint of the gusts he had felt up on the balcony of the Pengrig and certainly no signs of a storm. He entered his room, closed the door behind him and threw himself on the bed. He didn't want to sleep—he wanted to lie here and try to think of something he could do to help Ella—but exhaustion overcame him and soon he was dozing. When he awoke, the sun had gone down and dusk was closing in. He sat up on the bed and stared out of the window.

The tops of the conifers were swaying.

He switched on the light and saw a tray by the bed with some sandwiches and a glass of orange juice. Mum must have looked in around supper time and decided to let him sleep. He heard her voice downstairs, and Dad's, and wondered what they were talking about. There had clearly been no phone call. He reached for a sandwich, then stopped.

To the right of the tray was something gold. He stared for a moment, then saw it was the pendulum. He'd forgotten all about it since Sam dropped it in panic and ran from the room. He picked up the thread of hair and let the ring hang down. It was strange to think that this frail device could have spun so decisively when Sam's finger touched the Pengrig lighthouse on the map—yet for all that, it had chosen the wrong place. Suddenly an idea rushed through his mind.

He jumped off the bed, found the local map and spread it over the floor. There was the coastal path, there was the sea, there was the Pengrig lighthouse, or rather the hole in the map where Sam's finger had pushed through in his excitement. Fin stared at it, his hand tight round the pendulum. The whole thing seemed ridiculous yet somehow it now made sense. The pendulum could only pick up what was on the surface of the map and it had chosen the lighthouse; yet underneath the lighthouse, directly below it, was another place, and Sam's finger had plunged through the cliff itself to find it.

14

Ella sensed the gale long before it came. She sensed it in the stillness of the chamber when the boy left that morning; she sensed it in the calmness of the sea, the blue of the sky, the mewing of the gulls. She sensed it even when she doubted it was there; it was like a bubble growing within her, around her, everywhere. Now, as the light faded once more, the waves were growing, the wind was rising, the clouds were racing overhead—and she knew she was right.

The storm was about to break.

She sat on the flat rock down in the cave; cold, numb, frightened. She felt she was waiting for something but she didn't know what it was. Nothing made sense any more. She had almost lost track of who she was in the two days that she had been here. All she knew was that she was unwell, that she was dirty, that she hadn't eaten or drunk since the night she was first brought here, and that her mind was a freak-show of pictures that filled her with fear.

She stared over the water as it raced in towards her. The waves were growing more powerful by the minute and she would have to move back to the chamber soon or risk being washed off. She saw a shape moving in the entrance to the cave and stood up. It was the boy—there was no mistaking that massive figure in the dinghy—but something was wrong. He was rowing fast and his oar-strokes were short, splashy, hurried. He drew closer to the rock and looked up at her.

One glance at his face was enough. He was going to kill her. She turned and hurried up the tunnel, terror rushing through her. She knew there was no escape here but there was no escape anywhere and she had to run, had to do something. She reached the chamber and cowered in the far corner, staring towards the entrance. The boy soon appeared.

'Please,' she said. 'Whatever you're going to do—'

'Your brother,' he said. 'The little kid.' He walked forward and stopped in the centre of the chamber. To her surprise she saw he was trembling. 'What's his name?' he snapped.

'He . . . he . . . '

'What's his name?'

'Sam. He's . . . he's called Sam.'

The boy's face was dark with fury. She watched, shaking, trying to understand what had happened. He glared at her. 'What's he like, this Sam?'

'He's . . . he's . . . '

'What's he like?' he bellowed.

'He's . . . he's three years old and he . . . he likes playing games and things and he . . . ' She started crying. 'I don't know what to say. What do you want me to say? He's a little boy. He's like most little boys. No, he's . . . he's not like most little boys. He's different. He's—'

'Different?' The boy pounced on the word. 'How's he different?'

141

She pressed herself back against the wall. The boy bellowed at her again.

'How's he different?'

'He . . . he sees things. He hears things. I don't know, he's just . . . different.'

The boy turned and stared out through one of the gaps in the wall. She saw the features of his face moving in the failing light.

'I was wrong,' he said. 'I thought it would be OK to let you go but it's not. It would be a betrayal.' He turned to face her again and his eyes hardened. 'I'm sorry. I didn't want to do this but I've got to.'

And he strode towards her.

Fin fastened his lifejacket, pushed the dinghy clear of the slipway and rowed out towards the breakwater. At least there was a moon to see by, though the racing clouds kept distorting it. *Free Spirit* slipped astern, nuzzling at her mooring as the swell moved her. He cast an eye round the cove. It was deserted and he was glad of it. The last thing he needed right now was other people. He rounded the breakwater and felt the onshore waves drive against the boat, mostly long combers with hissing white crests but some shorter waves, too, that punched into the bow and thrust him back. He forced a way through them and pulled clear of the land.

He knew he had to be quick. The wind was rising all the time and soon the sea would be too dangerous to cross. Sam had been right about a storm coming. This one wasn't at full strength yet but it had a vicious smell already, just like the night Ella was taken. For the umpteenth time he asked himself what the hell he was doing. Even if Ella were in the chamber above the cave, and even if he managed to reach her, there was no guarantee that she'd be alone; he could still have that huge boy to deal with.

But perhaps that was it. He frowned. No—not perhaps. That *was* it. Why pretend that he regretted slipping out of the house without telling Mum and Dad when he knew he wanted it this way? There was a score to settle and it was his. He was the one who'd left Ella unguarded in the first place; he should be the one to bring her back—and if the boy were there, too, so much the better.

Gradually the headland drew closer, signals flashing from the automatic lighthouse at the top. He pulled on. There was the shadowy peak; there was the tower of the old Pengrig. He reached the base of the cliff and looked about him. The rocks were livid with foam. He felt his stomach tighten. Every part of him wanted to pull away now but he knew he could not. He had to go on, for Ella's sake. The cave opened before him like a whale's mouth; he wrestled the boat through the eddies towards it and suddenly he was inside.

Nothing he'd heard or read about this place prepared him for the horror of it. Rocks jeered at him like gargoyles, spray flew over him in icy showers; the sound of the sea was like thunder in his head. He searched for the flat rock he'd heard about. There it was, over to the right, and, close by, the tunnel to the upper chamber. He looked for a place to land.

There was only one spot the smugglers could have used, a slope at the end of the flat rock that formed a rough slipway to the top. He turned the dinghy and backwatered towards it, trying to resist the waves that were surfing him in, but it was no good. They were moving him too fast. He tried to pull back—in vain. The dinghy thudded against the wall of the cave. The jolt threw him into the stern of the boat. He floundered back to the thwart, unshipped the oars before he lost them over the side, and stretched out a hand for something to hold on to. But at that moment the next wave drove in.

The dinghy was lifted and flung back against the wall. He clung to the gunwales, struggling to stay in the boat. As the wave slipped back, he spotted a finger of rock in the wall close by. He seized it, slipped the painter round it and held tight. The boat stopped with a groan, the bow halfway up the slope. He leapt onto the slippery incline, released the painter, and scrambled with it to the top of the flat rock. As he did so, he saw the next wave rumble in.

He took a turn with the painter round a nub of rock, crouched by the entrance to the tunnel, and braced himself. The wave broke over the dinghy with a crash and thumped it against the wall again. He felt the painter tighten and a stream of water run past his feet; then the wave receded and the rope slackened in his hand.

But more waves were rolling in and he knew he would have to be quick before a larger one plucked him away. He freed the painter, hauled the dinghy to the top of the flat rock, and manhandled it round into the lower part of the tunnel. A few seconds later the next wave raced past the opening.

He leaned against the wall, breathing hard. There was no sign of another boat so the boy was probably not here. He pulled the torch from his oilskin pocket, switched it on and started up the tunnel, his heart now pounding with excitement. Ella had to be here. She had to be. Where else could she be? Sam had got everything right with the pendulum and this would surely be right, too. Just a few more steps and he'd be able to see her, hold her, tell her he was sorry, bring her home.

He hurried up the passageway as fast as he dared. His oilskins seemed to leak in a hundred places and he was shivering from the sodden clothing underneath but he didn't care. He was going to be with Ella soon. He knew it. He climbed on up the rocky stairway, the beam of the torch brightening the tunnel with an eerie glow, then finally he saw a pale light ahead. He switched off the torch, steeled himself in case of attack, and strode into the upper chamber.

All his hopes vanished in that moment. She was not here. No one was here. Tears rushed into his eyes as despair swallowed him once again; then he saw the shapes all around him. He wiped his eyes with the back of his hand, flicked on the torch and saw sandwich cartons, bottles of mineral water, boxes, and a towel. Over by the far wall was a bucket and close by his feet a couple of blankets. He knelt down, picked one of them up and shone the torch over it; and felt his excitement return.

Caught in the beam was a long golden hair.

15

The house looked like a spectral mansion; the two figures in the doorway, ghosts. One spoke. 'Where the hell have you been?'

It didn't sound like his father but he supposed it must be him. The other figure rushed forward and held him.

'Mum?' he said.

'Fin, it's past midnight. Where have you been? What's happened?'

He looked into her face but all he saw was the visage of the sea, black as a scream. 'Ella,' he mumbled, 'I . . . I know where she's been kept but . . .' The images still rolled in his mind but he blundered on. 'She's . . . she's not there any more. She's gone. She's—'

'Come inside,' said Mum.

'No—' He gripped her arm. 'We've got to act now. There's . . . there's something we can do to find her.'

Mum steered him into the house, closed the door behind them and turned to face him. 'We'll talk when you're dry. Off with the lifejacket.'

'But, Mum—'

'Lifejacket, darling.'

He hurriedly peeled it off, then the oilskins, aware of Dad watching him in silence by the door. Mum shook her head.

'You're soaked to the skin. Come with me.' Ignoring his protests, she took him by the hand, led him up to the bathroom and pushed him through the door. 'Strip off and towel down. Dump your wet things in the bath.' She fetched some dry clothes and dropped them on the floor. 'We'll be waiting out here,' she said and closed the door on him.

Somehow the routine of drying and dressing helped to relax him, but the visions of the sea and the cave did not let go and he was still trembling when he opened the door again. Mum and Dad were waiting outside. He opened his mouth at once to speak but Mum stopped him with a finger on his lips, led him down to the kitchen, and sat him in a chair.

'Now, then,' she said, pulling up a chair for herself next to him. 'Where have you been?'

He could see she was forcing herself to be calm and he tried to do the same. He saw Dad watching him grimly from the other side of the table.

'Well?' said Mum.

'I've been . . . ' He kept his eyes on Dad. 'I've been to the Pengrig cave and up the tunnel to the chamber.'

'What?' said Dad, stiffening.

'I thought . . . I thought Ella might be there. I took the dinghy. It's a bit . . . bashed up now. I'm sorry.' He paused, waiting for one of them to interrupt but they said nothing. He took a deep breath. 'I didn't tell either of you what I was doing because I knew you wouldn't let me go.'

'You're damn right,' said Dad.

'And you wouldn't have believed my reasons for thinking she was there. But you have to now and

147

we've got to try again. We can find her. I know we can.'

'What the hell are you talking about?'

'I made a pendulum. I got one of Ella's hairs and tied a ring to it and tried to find out where she was.'

'A pendulum?' said Dad. 'Is this a joke?'

'No.' Fin glared at him. 'You can find missing people with a pendulum. It's like dowsing for water.'

'It's hocus-pocus rubbish. Sounds like something Billy stuffed into your head.'

'I did get the idea from Billy—'

'Exactly.'

'Peter!' said Mum. 'Let him speak.' She touched Fin on the arm. 'Go on. Tell us what you did.' She gave Dad a frown. 'I've heard of pendulum dowsing.'

'So have I,' said Dad. 'But it doesn't alter the fact that it's hocus-pocus rubbish.'

'Go on, Fin,' said Mum.

'Billy doesn't know anything about Ella being missing but he's got this book and it tells you how you can get a map and run your finger over it and ask the pendulum questions, and if you do it right, you get answers and you can find people.'

'And did it work?'

'Not with me but it worked with Sammy.'

'Sam? You didn't involve him in this?'

'He wanted to have a go, and he was good at it. He was really good at it. I didn't work out about the cave at first. I got confused. The pendulum spun when Sammy put his finger on the Pengrig lighthouse so I went and checked it out. Didn't find anybody.' He looked at Dad. 'I was just coming back from there when I saw you talking to the tramp.'

Dad said nothing.

'But why the cave?' said Mum.

'I suddenly realized Sammy's finger could be pointing to what was underneath the lighthouse.'

She sighed. 'I still don't understand what possessed you to go to the cave. OK, you wanted to find Ella but you know how dangerous that place is and in a storm like this . . . ' She looked him hard in the face. 'You were very brave, Fin, but very irresponsible. You're lucky not to have been drowned.'

The images crowded back into his mind: the darkness of the cave, the waves throwing him back as he tried to launch the dinghy, the struggle to row clear, the battle to reach the shore. 'I know,' he said. 'I'm sorry—but at least I know she's been in the chamber.'

'What did you find there?'

'Blankets, and a bucket that's been used as a loo, and packs of sandwiches, and bottles of mineral water, and . . . ' He jumped up, ran to the hall and brought back his oilskin top, then pulled the sodden handkerchief from the pocket and carefully unfolded it. 'And this,' he said.

He held up the golden hair and Mum's eyes filled with tears. He put a hand on her shoulder. 'I'll be back,' he said. He sped up to his room, found the pendulum and the map, and raced back with them to the kitchen. 'See?' he said, holding up the pendulum. 'Identical hairs. She was definitely in the chamber. We've got to try the pendulum again.' He started to spread the map over the table but Dad reached down and stopped him.

'You said it didn't work with you.'

'It didn't. But Sammy—'

'I'm not having Sam involved again.'

'But—'

'That's final. Sam's really upset at the moment. The last thing he needs is parlour games.'

'Parlour games?' Fin frowned at him. 'What's worse, upsetting Sammy or losing Ella?'

'It's a bloody pendulum, for God's sake! You can't put all your faith in a gimmick.'

'But what if it works?' He thrust his face close to Dad's. 'What if it works? It found the hair, didn't it? Don't you want us to try anything?'

Mum stepped forward. 'That's enough.' She put her hands over Fin's cheeks and forced him to look at her. 'Go and get Sam but be as gentle as you can with him. He's very, very unstable. It's probably this business with Ella but I've got a feeling there's something else as well, though I don't know what it is.' She took her hands away from his face. 'Now go and get him.'

'And if he finds out where Ella is?'

'One thing at a time. Let's see what he can do first. Bring him down to the kitchen.' She saw Dad frowning at her and snapped at him. 'It's no use you looking at me like that! I don't want Sam involved any more than you do but Fin's right. We've got to try everything.' Dad looked angrily away and said nothing.

Fin hurried up the stairs to Sam's room. The little boy was tucked up in bed but not asleep.

'Sammy?'

Sam turned over and looked towards him, his eyes misty, almost frightening.

'She's gone,' he murmured. 'She's not going to play with me any more.'

'Who, Sammy? Ella?'

Sam didn't answer. His face looked pale in the light from the landing. Fin glanced down. 'What's this, Sammy?' he said. 'Teddy on the floor? That's not like you.' He bent down to pick Teddy up but Sam screamed at once.

'Leave him alone! Leave him alone!'

'Easy, Sammy.' Fin straightened up, leaving Teddy where he was. 'I won't touch him, not if you don't want me to.' He could see Sam was close to tears, close to something dangerous; and this was so uncharacteristic, not wanting Teddy with him. He tried to make his voice as gentle as he could. 'Don't you want Teddy with you, Sammy?'

'I want to see the girl with the golden hair.'

This was getting really disturbing. Sam could only mean Ella but why wasn't he using her name? Fin brushed the thought aside and returned to the matter in hand.

'Sammy? You remember that game we played in my room? We got a map and then we—'

'The pendlam game.'

'Good boy.' He ran a hand over Sam's brow. 'Sammy, I want to play it again right now. I want us to try and find Ella like we did before. Will you help me?'

He didn't expect much of a response but, to his surprise, Sam stirred right away. Fin turned back the sheet to help him get out.

'I'll do it myself,' said Sam.

'OK, Sammy.' He held out his hand and waited to see whether Sam would take it. He did and they walked out onto the landing. 'Let's play the pendulum game in the kitchen, Sammy. Mummy

151

and Daddy are down there and they want to see us do it.'

Sam stopped and looked up at him. 'But it's a secret.'

'I know, Sammy, but Mummy and Daddy really want to play it, too. I told them you wouldn't mind.'

Sam looked at him hard and for a moment seemed on the point of running back to his room, but then, to Fin's relief, he turned towards the stairs again and they walked down, hand in hand, to the kitchen. Mum and Dad were standing by the table, the map spread open upon it and the pendulum on top. There was an awkward silence, then Mum bent down and spread her arms for Sam. Sam let go of Fin's hand and stepped into her embrace.

'My love,' she said, pulling him to her. 'Thank you for helping us.'

'Sammy says we can play his pendulum game,' said Fin, 'as long as we remember it's a secret and don't tell anyone else about it.'

'Of course we won't,' said Mum. She looked up at Dad but he said nothing.

Fin bent down. 'Sammy, we're going to use the kitchen table this time, OK?'

'All right.'

He lifted Sam onto a chair by the table. 'Right, Sammy, let's show them how we play it.' He reached for the pendulum and held it out to Sam. 'Do you remember what to do? You move your finger over—'

'I know what to do.' Sam took the pendulum, climbed onto the table and crawled over the map. Fin watched uneasily, praying this would work. Sam was so strange at the moment it was hard to know whether he would manage it this time. Mum and Dad watched in a kind of frozen stillness as Sam held the end of the hair and let the ring hang down, then ran the forefinger of his other hand over the surface of the map.

'Show me where Ella is.' His voice rang out, as solemn as it had been the other times he had done this. Fin watched in awe. Sam had changed suddenly. The otherworldliness was still there but his eyes were fixed, intent. 'Show me where Ella is.'

The finger moved on but the pendulum hung still. Fin felt Dad twitch nearby. Their eyes met but neither spoke. He turned back to Sam, anxious now in case Dad said something and broke the spell, but his father remained silent and so did Mum, and the finger continued its journey, over Newquay and the nearby villages, then on towards Trevally, Sam's voice chanting its words like a mantra.

Dad twitched again. Fin knew what it meant, and he was feeling edgy, too. Sam's finger was moving over Trevally now but there was still no response from the pendulum. Perhaps the kidnapper had taken Ella out of Cornwall. Suddenly the finger strayed.

Mum spoke. 'Not that way, Sam. That blue bit's the sea.' But the finger kept on moving, away from the shore. 'Darling,' said Mum, 'she won't be there. That's the sea. That's—'

She gasped and looked round at Fin, but Fin was staring at the shaded blue space where Sam's finger now rested.

The pendulum was spinning.

16

The largest of the islands was surrounded by a ring of foam that glistened in the night as the waves drove in. The boy's energy was starting to fail but he struggled at the oars for the final stretch and somehow brought the dinghy to the sanctuary of the inlet.

'Grab the jetty,' he said.

She caught hold of it as they drew alongside.

'Climb out.'

She clambered up and walked as far as the rocks. She was shivering uncontrollably from the cold, the wet, the horrors of the boat journey, the fear of what lay ahead. She knew resistance was useless. If the boy had the will and the strength to row through seas as dangerous as these, nothing would stop him doing whatever he intended here. He hauled the dinghy up the rocks and turned towards her.

'Walk up the slope. Stop at the highest point.'

She set off, not daring to look behind. At the highest point of the island she stopped and turned. The boy was only a few feet away. She looked at him towering over her.

'Why are you going to kill me?' she said.

He turned away and gazed over the water. 'You know what they used to call these islands?' She didn't answer. 'They called them the Furies,' he said.

154

'I always thought that was a good name. But you probably don't know who the Furies were.' He looked round at her. 'They were merciless old women who punished people who'd committed crimes in their own families. And do you know how they punished them? They filled them with guilt so terrible it made them lose their reason.'

'But why should I feel guilt?'

He pulled a gun from his oilskin pocket and studied it. 'Friend of mine gave me this,' he said. 'Guy I shared a doorway with in London. Never thought I'd have to use it.' He looked back at her. 'The guilt doesn't belong to you. It belongs to someone else. But you're the price that has to be paid for it.'

She took a step back. 'What's happened to you? What's made you like this?'

'Sit down,' he said. She didn't move. He nodded to a rock. 'I said sit down.' She sat down on it, her eyes still on the gun. He sat on another nearby. 'I'll tell you a story,' he said.

Sam sat up in bed with a start. The little girl was standing by the far wall, her golden hair and white dress bright against the darkness. She smiled at him and her voice spoke inside his head.

Can you hear the storm?

He could hear it. It frightened him but it was exciting, too. She walked to the door, then turned and beckoned.

Let's go and catch it.

He climbed out of bed. He was very tired, especially after getting up earlier to play the pendlam game, but he was so pleased to see the little girl again. He'd thought she was never going to come back. She put a finger to her lips.

Come on.

He followed her out onto the landing. The wind sounded very loud but the little girl didn't seem scared at all. She stopped at the top of the stairs and turned to face him.

We must be very quiet.

He heard noises down in the sitting room. It could only be Mummy. Fin and Daddy had rushed out of the house after the pendlam game and hadn't come back. He wondered where they were.

The little girl moved nearer and looked him in the face. She had never been so close before and he thought for a moment she was going to let him touch her. He wanted to so much but he didn't dare. She always moved away when he tried and then he felt silly. She smiled.

It'll be dawn soon. Let's go outside and play.

'We can play here,' he said. But she shook her head.

I know a better place.

'I don't want to go to the lighthouse again.'

It'll be fun.

'Can't we catch the storm here?'

Don't be silly. Come on.

He looked at her, unsure what to do. He didn't want to go down the coastal path again but he didn't want to lose the little girl either. He felt sure she'd never come back if he didn't go with her.

'I want to get Teddy,' he said.

All right, but hurry up.

He ran back to his room and fetched Teddy. That

156

felt better. He'd forgotten him last time he played with the little girl. He hurried back to the landing and they stole downstairs. The little girl stopped outside the sitting room, looked round at him and put the finger to her lips again. He peeped round the door. Mummy was over by the far wall with her back to him, dusting the ornaments in the cabinet.

But she was doing it very strangely. Usually she hummed when she did this and took lots of time with each thing but this time she wasn't humming at all. She was just picking things up, dusting them a bit, and then putting them back somewhere else, or holding them for ages and staring into space before putting them back without even dusting them. He heard the little girl's voice again.

Hurry up or we won't get away.

He looked round and saw she was gone. But he knew where he'd find her. Sure enough, she was waiting by the back door. She nodded towards it.

Open it.

It was easy this time because the door was already unlocked and the bolt wasn't across. He turned the handle and the wind pushed the door against him so hard he nearly fell over. The little girl gave a chuckle.

Let's go.

And she skipped through into the garden. Somehow he pulled the door after him and closed it. It was still dark outside but the corners of the sky were growing brighter. The wind was cool and made his pyjama top flap like a sail. He tucked it in and looked round for the little girl. She was running across the lawn and the sound of her laughter rippled through him. He held Teddy tight and raced after her. To his relief, she stopped at the gate and waited for him. He caught her up, desperate not to lose sight of her for a moment, but she was already fidgeting to be off again.

Come on. Open the gate and let's go.

'Promise you won't run away.'

Open the gate.

He pulled open the gate and she tore off up the lane. 'Don't run away!' he called but she seemed to fly ahead, not looking back. He stood there, terrified of the storm. 'Please don't run away!'

Come to the coastal path.

'Can't we play here?'

Come to the coastal path.

'I don't want to go there. It's scary.'

Come to the coastal path.

She disappeared from view. He bolted up the lane, calling for her to stop, but she didn't. She ran on, always out of sight, her voice taunting him.

I'm just ahead. I'm just ahead.

'Where?'

He heard her laugh again. He wished she'd play properly. He hated it when she made fun of him. He clutched Teddy and stumbled on, straining for a glimpse of her. The wind grew stronger, colder, louder.

'Where are you?' he called.

Just ahead of you.

But still there was no sign of her. He reached the fork and ran on down the track towards the cliffs, the ground hard under his bare feet. The sea opened before him. It was covered with silver crests and looked fierce and beautiful. 'Where are you?' he called.

Over here, over here.

And there she was, just beyond the bracken by the signpost to the coastal path. She waved and started to move off in the direction of Pengrig.

'Wait,' he said.

Come on. Let's go and catch the storm.

'Can't we do it here? I don't want to go to the lighthouse.'

It'll be fun.

'It's scary.'

Don't be silly. We're only going to play.

And she ran off towards Pengrig. He stared after her. She seemed to move like a bird and she wasn't frightened of anything. But he was. No matter how much he wanted to be with her, he was scared, really scared. He heard her voice calling again.

Come on. Don't you want to be with me?

He squeezed Teddy into his chest and sped after her.

It was dawn when the boy finished speaking and for Ella everything had changed. But there was no time to think. He stood up and looked down at her.

'That's enough talking.'

'Please—'

'I said that's enough! There's nothing more to say. I don't want to hear anything from you.'

'But—'

'I said I don't want to hear anything from you.'

'Please, I—'

'Shut up!' He was bawling at her now but there was desperation in his voice, too, and even a touch of fear. 'Don't talk to me! Don't say anything! I don't want to hear from you!' He glared at her, both hands tight round the gun. 'You've got to die!' he shouted. 'You've got to! It's the right thing!'

'But—'

'No!' He screwed his eyes together. 'I'm not going to listen to you!'

'But—'

'Shut up! Please!' He lowered his voice and went on through gritted teeth, his eyes still tightly closed. 'Don't speak to me. Don't say anything. Don't . . . don't make me like you.'

He stood there, his chest heaving, his face tight with pain, then suddenly he opened his eyes and raised the gun. She gave a scream, jumped to her feet, and scrambled away over the rocks. She heard him thumping after her.

17

Fin stood next to Dad in the wheelhouse and craned forward as *Free Spirit* struggled to pull away from the land. Dawn had broken to reveal a ferocious seascape. The storm was now at its height and great billows were rolling in from the ocean. The boat punched into them through a chaos of spray. Dad bellowed at him. 'Take a bearing on the cliff and tell me if we're making any headway.'

He looked over at Pengrig. 'We're moving, but not very fast.'

Dad grunted and hunched over the wheel. Fin peered ahead but with the mad motion of the bows it was hard to see much. Wave followed wave, throwing them about with ugly malevolence, yet somehow the headland passed to starboard and the islands hove into view round the point.

They drew closer with painful slowness, the waves fighting the boat for every yard. Fin pulled out the binoculars and focused them on the two smaller islands. He didn't expect to see anyone—Sam's finger had clearly pointed to the largest of the three—but it was worth checking. All he saw was rocks and gulls.

'See anything?' said Dad.

'No.'

'I still can't believe we're doing this. All for a bloody pendulum.'

Fin said nothing. He knew the pendulum would be right. It was not a question of where she was but why—and were they too late? They moved on to the third island and he focused the binoculars again. Still nothing but rocks and birds. He found his hands trembling. She had to be here—and the boy. Yes, he wanted the boy, too.

'Any sign?' said Dad.

'No, but they'll be there.'

'We'll take a look in the inlet and if there's a boat there, we'll try and land—unless it's too dangerous.' Dad stared round at the whitecaps. 'At least it's under the lee of the island so we should have some protection, but if it's too rough in there, I'm not going in.'

He turned the wheel. It took a moment for *Free Spirit* to respond but gradually she came round under the shoulder of the island. The wind pressure eased at once, though smaller, sharper waves still smacked into the side of the boat. The inlet opened before them. Inside, pulled up on the rocks by the jetty, was a dinghy.

'I know that boat,' said Dad. 'It's Howard Spencer's tender. He had it stolen a while back.' He stared over the island. 'Can you see anyone?'

'No.'

Dad eased off the power. 'We'll go in but I don't like it. The water's rough as hell in there.' He frowned. 'We'll go alongside the jetty. Put the fenders over the side and get the mooring lines ready.'

'How many?'

'Four. Bow line, stern line, and two springs.

162

But be careful. I don't want you going over the side.'

Fin hurried out on deck. Even here in the more sheltered water of the inlet the wind was fierce and he had to hold on tight as he made his way about the boat. He lowered the fenders over the side, prepared the mooring lines, and waited in the bow as they moved closer to the jetty.

The sound of a gunshot tore down on the wind.

Fin looked round in alarm and saw from Dad's face that he had heard it, too. He picked up the bow line and braced himself to jump onto the jetty. Dad leaned out of the window of the wheelhouse and bawled at him.

'Don't run off! Stay and moor the boat!'

But Fin took no notice. He leapt onto the jetty, made fast the bow line, and raced off toward the rocks.

'Wait!' shouted Dad. 'He's got a gun!'

But Fin didn't wait. He couldn't wait. The boat didn't matter. Only Ella mattered. If she was dead, then he didn't want to live either. He didn't deserve it anyway. But he would take the boy with him. He scrambled over the rocks until he reached the highest point of the island, then looked down around him. There was no sign of anyone.

'Ella!' he shouted. 'Ella!'

He whirled round, searching in all directions. Back on the jetty he saw Dad furiously making fast the other mooring lines. He turned and ran his eye over the northern tip of the island; and then he saw them: two heads above a boulder down by the water's edge. They must be leaning with their backs against it, facing the spray. Her head was tipped to one side. The boy must have shot her.

He tore over the rocks towards them, his rage rising like a flood. He knew he would kill or be killed and it didn't seem to matter which now. He leapt from rock to rock, seeing only the two heads above the boulder, hers and his—and then only his. Hers was still there, lifeless, unmoving, but the other head was the one he wanted. He reached the boulder, put his foot on it and leapt over in front of them. 'You bastard,' he said, advancing on the boy. 'I'm going to kill you.'

'He's already dead,' said a voice.

He stopped and stood there, spray showering him from the sea. It was Ella who had spoken, though he hardly recognized the voice. He stared at her. She had not moved. Her head was still tipped to the side but she did not appear to be injured. She was cradling a gun in her lap. He looked back at the boy and saw blood round his temple.

Dad arrived a few moments later and knelt down. 'Ella, it's us. Everything's OK.' He looked her over, then, with some hesitation, took the gun from her and placed it out of reach. She moved her head slightly but did not look at them. Dad glanced at the boy as though to reassure himself there was no danger, then pulled Ella to him. 'My love.' She didn't resist but didn't hold him either. He kissed her head. 'Thank God you're all right. What happened?'

She didn't answer. Her eyes were glazed, her arms limp. Fin looked back at the boy. He was indeed huge and intimidating, yet the face was strangely mild, even with the blood spattered over it. But Fin felt no sympathy for him. 'Dad,' he said, 'we've got to get her home.'

'I must check the boy first.'

'He's dead.'

Dad reached out and felt the boy's pulse. 'He's not but he will be if we don't act fast. Run to the boat and get my mobile. It's in the starboard locker.'

Fin looked at Ella. He didn't want to leave her for a moment. Her face was white and she was shivering. Why should he care about the boy who had caused all this?

'Fin!' Dad snapped at him. 'Quick!'

Reluctantly he hurried back to the inlet. *Free Spirit* was bumping against the jetty but with the fenders and mooring lines in place she seemed in no danger. He jumped aboard, found the mobile phone, and raced back, his mind black with worry.

What had happened? Clearly the boy had planned to kill her on the island, yet somehow she must have wrestled the gun from him and shot him instead. It didn't seem possible. How could Ella—sweet little Ella who dissolved in tears if she trod on a beetle— bring herself to point a gun at someone and pull the trigger? And what had the boy done to her to make her capable of such a thing?

He found her still slumped against the rock and Dad bent over the boy, pressing a handkerchief to his temple. He held out the phone. Dad took it and stood up. 'Look after Ella,' he said and walked back a few yards, away from the spray.

Fin knelt down and put an arm round her. She felt so fragile. 'El?' he said. She didn't move, either towards him or away. She simply stared towards the boy. He pulled her gently closer. 'I'll take care of you,' he said.

He heard Dad shouting into the phone, his voice just audible against the crash of the waves. 'Air ambulance . . . Yes . . . Peter Parnell . . . I'm on a mobile . . . 01764 509616 . . . Polvellan, Trevally but I'm not there at the moment . . . I'm on the biggest of the Pengrig islands . . . My son Fin and my daughter Ella and a boy . . . He's been shot . . . Yes, still alive but I don't know how long he's going to last . . . What? . . . His name?'

Fin felt Ella stiffen in his arms. She looked at Dad and spoke. 'His name's Ricky Prescott.'

Her voice was hard, her eyes red. Dad's face seemed to drain of colour. He watched her for a moment, as though waiting for her to speak again, but she let her head fall to the side and said no more. He turned and walked away out of hearing. Fin drew Ella to him again. Speaking those few words seemed to have freed something in her and she was crying now. He stroked her arm, murmuring whatever he could think of to say, though he knew she probably heard none of it. But he sensed she was glad he was there. Dad came back.

'The air ambulance people are coming,' he said.

'Are they going to contact the police?'

'Yes.' Dad frowned and knelt down to check the boy's pulse again.

'Is he still alive?' said Fin.

'Just about.' He reached out with the handkerchief but it was covered in blood.

'Take mine,' said Fin.

'Thanks.' Dad took it and held it to the boy's wound again. Fin watched, still holding Ella close.

'Are they going to take El to the hospital, too?'

Ella stirred in his arms again. 'I'm not going to the hospital,' she said. Fin looked at her, surprised at the violence in her voice. She spoke again. 'I'm not going to the hospital. I'm going home.'

'It's OK.' He tried to smile at her. 'We won't let anyone take you away. The boy'll go to the hospital but you're coming back with us. Right, Dad?'

Dad was still bent over the boy but he heard and looked round. 'Right.'

Ella said nothing but seemed reassured. Fin leaned his head closer to hers. 'I'll be with you all the time. I won't leave you for a second. You're going to come through this and before you know it you'll be happy again, and this will all slip away into the past and it won't hurt you any more.'

He knew the words sounded stupid but he didn't know what else to say. Dad looked round at him, then turned back to the boy and muttered something. But Fin caught the words.

'The past doesn't let go that easily.'

Sam was more scared than he'd ever been. Daylight had come but the storm was like a wild beast with sea thrashing, bracken swaying, wind whirling. The little girl was gone. He didn't know where she was and she hadn't spoken for some time, but she'd run towards Pengrig and so he followed, hoping he would find her. The lighthouse appeared ahead and the voice spoke again at last.

Bet you can't find me.

He stopped and looked around him. The voice gave a giggle.

Not there. You're a long way away. Come as far as the lighthouse.

He ran up to it and stopped by the fence. 'Where are you?'

Well, I'm not out to sea.

He spun round and saw her standing by the bracken. She was laughing at him.

Come on. Jump up and catch the storm.

He looked round at the cliff-edge close by.

'I don't want to,' he said, but the little girl laughed again.

Come on, do what I do and catch the storm. And she started jumping up at the sky, her arms outstretched.

'Don't,' he said, looking round at the edge again. 'Don't.'

She took no notice. She skipped over to him and started to run round him, round him, round him, jumping up as she did so and clutching at the sky, and giggling inside his head.

Catch the storm! Catch the storm!

'Stop!'

Catch the storm!

He whirled round with her, dizzy, scared. 'Please stop!'

She ran off towards the bracken. He stopped whirling round and stood still, choking back the tears, Teddy held tight against his cheek. 'Where are you?' he called.

Here.

And then he saw her, half-hidden in the bracken, pulling a face at him; then she disappeared again.

'Don't!'

She ran out, pulled another face, and ran back into the bracken.

'What are you teasing me for?'

You're scared of the storm.

'I'm not!'

You are.

'Where are you?'

Here. And she ran out again, pulled another face, and disappeared once more.

'Come back!'

Scared of the storm! You're scared of the storm!

'I want to go home.'

Scared of the storm!

'Where are you? I can't see you.'

Up here. Look.

But still he saw nothing.

Up here.

'Please come out,' he said.

I am out. Look.

And now he saw her, much further up in the bracken, waving to him. He felt a rush of relief but it quickly vanished as she disappeared again.

'Don't,' he said. 'Please don't hide any more.'

Come and find me.

'Please.'

Come and find me.

He hated the way her voice mocked him. She knew he was scared, she knew he wanted to be with her. She was playing but not the way he wanted.

'Please,' he said.

No answer. He started to whimper, then the voice spoke again.

Come into the bracken and you'll find me.

He didn't want to go into the bracken but he took a few steps in. To his surprise it felt safer than the open cliff top, though he wished the leaves would stop waving about in the wind. He couldn't see the little girl. She spoke again.

You've got to come in much further than that.

He walked on, pushing the stems to the side. The ground started to rise but bracken still covered him like an umbrella. He climbed for what seemed a long time, then the voice came again.

You're warm. You're near.

'I can't see you.'

You're not looking.

'I am.'

Over here.

He caught a shadowy movement a few feet away. It was the girl, scampering off again. He ran after her as fast as he could. 'Please wait for me,' he called.

No answer.

'Please.'

Again no answer. He stopped, listening for her voice, but all he heard was the wind and the sea as he stood there in the strange, twisting forest. Something was wrong. He could sense it. This wasn't teasing any more. He stared up through the bracken and saw clouds ripping the sky in fiery swathes. The lantern of the Pengrig was a dark, bloody gold. Suddenly the little girl screamed inside him.

'Where are you?' he shouted back.

She didn't answer. She only screamed again deep within him, a scream of a kind he had never heard before and never wanted to hear again. It was as though he were screaming himself, and suddenly he was, screaming with her as though her voice were his voice. Then he saw her, just a few feet from him, scrambling through the bracken towards the lighthouse.

'Wait!' he shouted, but she took no notice and ran on, out of her mind with terror. He stumbled after her, still clutching Teddy. She was running as though blind, thrusting the bracken desperately to the side. He followed, calling to her to stop, but she ran on, still screaming. They broke clear of the bracken, the girl just ahead of him, and she raced round the lighthouse fence towards the cliff-edge.

'Stop!' he shouted but still she ran on, arms flailing, head back. The sea yawned before them. 'Stop!' he shouted. 'Stop!'

Then suddenly she wasn't there.

'No!' He shrieked into the wind and kept on running. She couldn't be gone. She couldn't. He heard her voice calling him from below and pelted towards the edge. The land fell away and the sea opened beneath him.

18

Fin watched the helicopter wheel away into the sky, carrying the body of Ricky Prescott—and the gun—back to shore. The air ambulance people had wasted little time but it would obviously be touch and go with the boy. Not that Fin cared. He turned and looked at Ella. She was still slumped against the rock. She had flared up when the medics tried to persuade her to let them airlift her to the hospital rather than go home in the boat but now she was silent again, her eyes dark and withdrawn.

'Come on,' he said. 'I'll help you back to the boat.' He bent down to pick her up but she pushed his arms aside.

'She wants to walk,' said Dad.

'I know that.' Fin shot an angry glance at him. He felt Ella take his hand and tug slightly, as though she wanted him to pull her up. He drew her to her feet and the three of them made their way back to the boat. *Free Spirit* was still bumping against the jetty but seemed to have suffered no damage. Dad climbed aboard and held out his hand for Ella. She ignored it, climbed aboard by herself, and went straight down to the cabin. Dad frowned and looked up at Fin.

'Sort the mooring lines, can you?'

'Which ones first?'

'Springs, then the stern line, then the bow line.

But wait till I've got the engine going before you do anything.'

He started the engine and let it run for a few minutes, then nodded up to the jetty. Fin cast off the lines, jumped aboard, and brought in the fenders. They set off out of the inlet and turned towards the cove. The violence of the sea hit them the moment they reached open water. The motion of the boat was more frightening than ever now. Where before they had been straining into the wind and the onshore seas, now both hurled them towards the land, the waves no longer smashing over the foredeck but lifting the stern and trying to force the bows off course. Dad gripped the wheel tight as he struggled to stop the boat broaching round broadside to the oncoming rollers. Fin left him alone to concentrate and hurried down to the cabin.

Ella was sitting on the nearest bunk, her eyes tightly closed. He sat next to her, unsure what to do, but she leaned towards him and rested her head on his shoulder.

'El,' he said, 'I'm so sorry.'

She slipped her arms round him and held him to her, and he held her, one arm round her waist, the other gripping the side of the bunk as the boat lurched this way and that. Before long Dad called down. 'Fin, I need you up here.'

He looked her in the face. 'I won't be long, OK? I'll be right back.' He joined Dad up in the wheelhouse and to his surprise saw that they were almost back at the cove. The breakwater was just ahead and the tender was clearly visible, bobbing on the mooring beyond. Dad pointed.

'What the hell's he doing there?'

Fin stared. Billy was standing at the end of the slipway, looking forlorn in the grey morning light, but beckoning furiously. They motored round the breakwater and picked up the mooring. Dad switched off the engine and hailed the shore.

'What's happened?'

Billy shouted something but his words didn't reach them against the wind. Dad roared back. 'Wait till we get ashore!' He turned to Fin. 'Go and get Ella. We'll tidy up the boat later.'

He fetched Ella from below and they climbed down into the dinghy. Dad joined them, took the oars and rowed them to the slipway. Billy started gabbling at once.

'It's Sam,' he said breathlessly. 'He's gone missing.'

'Christ!' said Dad. 'That's all we need.'

'Mrs Parnell rang us. We're all out looking and she said I was to come down here and wait for you to get back. And she's phoned the police.' Billy glanced at Ella. 'She told us about you. I'm really sorry.'

'Everybody out of the boat,' said Dad. 'Quick!'

They climbed onto the slipway and pulled the dinghy to the rack, then raced up to the top of the cliff and down the track to the fork. Mum was hurrying up the lane towards them. 'Ella!' she shouted and ran forward. 'My love, my love!' She clasped her tightly to her. 'Thank God you're safe but now Sam's gone missing.'

'Mum,' said Fin. 'I—' He checked himself. 'Billy, where are the others?'

'Mum and Dad are looking for Sam in the fields round Polvellan. Angie's waiting at the house to tell the police where we are when they get here.'

'Well, can you go back and help them? We'll check out the coastal path.'

'Sam won't be up there. It's too scary a place for a little kid.'

'Maybe, but can you go anyway?'

Billy looked at him, then shrugged. 'OK, I get it. You don't want me around. I'll see you later.' And before anyone could answer, he ran off down the track. Fin turned back to the others.

'Come on. I know where Sam'll be.'

He started to run. Dad called to him to wait but he took no notice. There was no time to waste. He felt no guilt about getting rid of Billy. This was a family matter and they needed to sort it out by themselves. The rest of the world would be involved soon enough. He reached the coastal path, checked to make sure the others were following, then raced on towards Pengrig. The wind was still gusting strongly and the sea was a savage white. He reached the lighthouse and stopped by the fence, his eyes searching all around. But there was no sign of Sam anywhere. The others arrived.

'Oh, God,' said Mum. 'I can't bear the thought of him coming up here.' She looked at Fin. 'What makes you think he's come this way?'

He bit his lip. 'Sammy ran out again on Tuesday night.'

'What?'

'And he came up here. I caught up with him and brought him back.'

'Why didn't you tell us?'

'I didn't want to get him into trouble.'

'You wouldn't have got him into trouble. What were you thinking of, Fin?'

'I'm sorry. I'm sorry.'

'You should never have kept it from us. What was he doing when you saw him?'

'Running along the path and calling to someone to wait for him. I didn't see anyone with him.'

'Go and see if he's further down the path. Hurry! We'll have a look round here.'

He bolted off, struggling with guilt and now terrible fear. To find Ella and then lose Sam. He ran a few hundred yards down the path, looking frantically about him, but there was no sign. 'Sammy!' he shouted. 'Sammy!' His voice was carried away in the storm. He tore back to the others, dreading the thought of facing Mum again. But he knew he had to tell her all he'd seen.

She was with Dad, searching the bracken close to the lighthouse. Ella was standing stiffly behind them, as still as the lighthouse, her eyes fixed on Dad. She seemed frighteningly remote. Mum looked up from the bracken, saw him and rushed out.

'Anything?'

Fin shook his head and she slumped to the ground, moaning.

'Mum.' He knelt down. 'There's something I didn't tell you.'

'What?'

He felt Dad and Ella move closer to listen.

'When I saw Sammy up here, he was . . . he was running like crazy towards the edge of the cliff.'

Her face turned pale. 'Which part of the cliff?' she said.

He nodded to the right of the lighthouse. She stared round at it, then slowly stood up. 'You and Ella are to wait here,' she said. 'You're not to go any closer to the edge, you understand? Your father and I will look over.'

Mum and Dad inched their way towards the edge, bracing themselves as the wind thrashed round them. Fin watched, clenching and unclenching his fists, and still battling with guilt. Nearby he sensed Ella shaking; he glanced round and saw her face was dark, angry, bitter. It scared him to see her like this. He looked back at Mum and Dad. They were on hands and knees now, crawling the last few feet. They reached the edge and peered over.

Mum's scream flew back on the wind.

Fin and Ella hurried forward. Dad pulled back from the edge and held out his hand. 'Go back! Don't come any closer!' They carried on. He scrambled to his feet and ran towards them. 'I said don't go any closer!'

They stopped, both glaring at him.

'We've got to see,' said Fin. 'We've got to see.' He saw Mum pull back from the edge and sit up, her face wreathed in tears. 'Mum!' he called. He pushed past Dad and hurried towards her. She waved him back but he took no notice, threw himself to the ground and crawled forward until his face was over the edge. Far below him the rocks were awash with foam, plumes of spray rising as the waves thundered in. He felt Ella crawl beside him and look down.

'Oh, no,' she murmured.

'Where?' he said. 'I can't see.'

She pointed to the right and he gasped. Forty feet down from the top of the cliff, wedged in a tangle of jutting rocks, was a teddy bear. He felt a sick pain inside him. It didn't seem possible that Teddy could cling on through the storm while Sam—little Sam— was gone. But even as he watched, a stronger gust threw itself against the cliff and suddenly Teddy was falling. For a moment he seemed to hang there, suspended in the storm like a strange lost creature, then all Fin saw was boiling sea.

He knew then that Sam was dead. No one could survive in waters like these. Nearby he heard Mum and Ella weeping and soon he was crying himself. 'It's my fault,' he said. 'It's my fault. Everything's my fault.'

'It's not your fault!' snapped Ella. He looked round at her, startled at the fierceness in her voice, but she turned and glared at Dad, who was standing behind them, staring down at the sea. 'It's his fault,' she said, 'not yours.'

'What did you say?' said Mum, looking sharply at her. 'Ella?'

But Ella didn't answer. Instead she jumped to her feet and squared up to Dad. 'Tell them!' she said.

'I don't know what you're talking about.'

'Tell them!'

Fin and Mum stood up together. 'Peter?' said Mum. 'What's this about?'

'I don't know,' said Dad.

'You do!' Ella snarled at him. 'It's punishment. I was meant to die but Sam's paid the price instead!'

'Ella.' Dad reached out to touch her but she drew back. 'Ella, you're overwrought. You're in shock. You're—'

'Why won't you admit it?'

Mum put an arm round her. 'Ella, easy. What's this about?'

'Ask him.'

'About what?'

'About Lindy Prescott.'

'Look,' said Dad, 'this isn't the time for talking.' He pulled out his mobile. 'We've got to report Sam missing and get some help out here. He might just still be alive.'

'But he's dead!' said Ella. 'He's dead!'

Fin stiffened suddenly. 'No, he's not.'

Far up the slope, deep in the bracken, was a small movement of hair. Fin charged towards it, thrusting the fronds aside as he ploughed his way upwards. No wonder they hadn't seen Sam. He was far above the coastal path. He must have dropped Teddy over the cliff and crawled up into the bracken in fright. Why he had come to Pengrig in the first place was still a mystery and maybe always would be but that didn't matter right now.

'Sammy!' he shouted.

Sam didn't turn, didn't stir. Only his hair moved as the wind whipped over it. As Fin drew closer, he saw that the boy's face was pressed into the ground. Panic seized him again, but then Sam looked round.

'Sammy, it's me, it's me!'

And suddenly Sam was in his arms and they were flopped together in the bracken, Sam clinging to him, eyes tightly closed. He was crying softly, his face buried in Fin's neck. Mum and Ella arrived and threw themselves down.

'Is he hurt?' said Mum.

'Don't think so,' said Fin. 'Just upset. Do you want to take him?'

Mum nodded and Fin made to pass Sam over but the little boy screamed at once.

'Keep him with you,' said Mum. 'We'll wait here till he settles.'

And so they waited, Fin holding Sam, Mum

holding Ella. Dad arrived and stood there, watching Sam in silence; then his eyes met Ella's and he turned away, wandered back down to the lighthouse, and stood by the cliff-edge, gazing over the sea. A few minutes later Mum leaned forward and looked Sam over.

'I think he's sleeping,' she said to Fin.

'Yeah. He's more knackered than scared now.'

'Keep him with you, can you? Don't let go of him.' She reached a hand out to Ella. 'Come on. Let's sort this business out.'

And she walked with Ella down through the bracken towards the lighthouse. Fin followed, holding Sam tightly to him and marvelling at the way the boy slept, seemingly unaware of the wind on his body or the sound of the surf crashing below them. They reached the path and Mum led them towards the edge of the cliff. Dad was still standing there, facing the sea, but he turned as they approached and looked straight at Mum.

'Lindy Prescott worked at the Newquay store fourteen years ago,' he said.

She looked him over in silence for a moment, then frowned. 'I thought I remembered the name. I've heard it somewhere else, too, but I can't remember where. Maybe you're going to tell me.' Dad said nothing. She looked him over again, then turned to Ella. 'But what I really want to know is where you've heard it.'

'From Ricky,' she said.

'Ricky?'

'Her son. The boy who kidnapped me.' Ella threw Dad a baleful glance. 'He told me everything on the island—everything.'

'I don't know what you're accusing me of,' said Dad. 'Lindy Prescott worked at the Newquay store just after it opened. I don't remember her that well. It's a long time ago, for God's sake. Young woman, early twenties. She worked at the checkout. She only stayed with us a few weeks, then she moved on and I never saw her again. I remember her telling me she had a little boy about a year old and that the kid's father had dumped her a couple of months earlier. I don't know what lies she's told her son about me and what he's told you but—'

'She didn't tell him anything.' Ella glowered at him. 'He hardly even remembers her. She died in a car accident when he was six.'

'I didn't know that.'

'Well, you do now. Ricky was taken into care. He told me about it. He lived in foster homes all over the country. One of them was by the sea somewhere in Norfolk and he learnt to sail and row, but then he had to move to another place where he was unhappy. He ran away when he was twelve and lived rough in London for three years, then he decided to come back to Cornwall for the first time since his mother died. And he met a man called Kelman on a street corner in Newquay.'

Dad's face darkened and he looked at Mum again. Her lips were tightly closed but her eyes never left him.

'It's the man Fin saw me talking to in the lane,' he said.

Still she didn't speak. Dad watched her uneasily.

'He's a piece of scum,' he said. 'You might have heard his name, too. I'm sure I mentioned it. He worked at the Newquay store the same time Lindy Prescott was there. I should never have taken him on

181

but I needed the labour and he was just about employable in those days. He was bad news from the start. Drunk, abusive, dishonest. I sacked him after a few weeks and he's had a grudge against me ever since.'

He paused, his eyes still searching Mum's face as though he were waiting for her to speak, but still she remained silent.

'He followed me around for months after I got rid of him, threatening this, that, and the other. I didn't tell you about it. I didn't want to worry you and I thought I could handle it on my own. Then he disappeared and I thought he'd gone for good but he turned up again a few weeks ago and started threatening me all over again. I don't think he's violent but he'd certainly fabricate a story against me if he thought he could make it stick. I don't know what he's told this Ricky Prescott but you can be certain it's a pack of lies.'

Mum spoke at last; and her voice was like ice. 'So it was a checkout girl.'

'What?'

'I always wondered who it was.' She looked him over in disgust. 'And every time I asked you, you said there wasn't anyone.'

'There wasn't.'

'Don't lie to me, Peter. It's written all over your face and it was then. I should have trusted my instincts and pushed you till you admitted it, but I was stupid enough to believe what you told me instead.'

'Look, I'm not putting up with this.' Dad took a step towards the coastal path but Mum seized him by the arm.

'Don't you dare walk away!' She thrust her face close to his. 'Ella's been through hell because of something you've done and the least she deserves— the least I deserve—is the truth.'

'All right!' Dad wrenched his arm free but didn't move away. He stood there for a moment, staring towards the lighthouse, then suddenly put a hand over his eyes. 'All right,' he muttered. 'All right, all right, all right.'

Fin watched tensely, Sam still sleeping in his arms. Close by, he sensed Ella trembling. Dad breathed out hard.

'I know it was wrong. I haven't got an excuse. I was mixed up. The new store wasn't making money. I'd just become a magistrate and I didn't think I was doing it very well. You were pregnant with Ella and you were all wrapped up with that and not very interested in me and . . . and Lindy was there. She was young and pretty and uncomplicated, and she was miserable. Her partner had just dumped her. And there I was.'

Mum slapped him hard in the face. 'You bastard!'

Fin gave a start and heard a gasp from Ella. Dad put a hand up to protect his face.

'I know,' he said to Mum. 'I'm sorry. It was wrong.'

'You're damn right it was wrong,' she said. 'And where does this Kelman come into it?'

'He was besotted with Lindy. Followed her round like a lapdog. She kept telling him she wasn't interested but he went on harassing her. That was another reason why I sacked him. But it was just the start of the trouble.'

183

A gull rose screaming on the wind and soared away over the lighthouse.

'The affair only lasted a few weeks. We both knew it wasn't going anywhere. Lindy left the store and I never saw her again. Then Kelman stopped me in the street. Said he'd had a lot of time on his hands since I sacked him so he'd taken up photography. And he pulled out some pictures he'd taken.'

Mum shook her head. 'You idiot.'

'They weren't anything sensational but they were enough to show two people who were more than just friends.'

'So he started blackmailing you.'

'Yes.'

'And like a spineless coward you paid him.'

'I couldn't bear the thought of losing you.'

'Don't give me that,' Mum snapped at him. 'You couldn't face the possibility of a scandal. Losing your reputation as a pillar of the community.'

'That, too, but it was the thought of losing you most of all. I promise. And I didn't want Fin and the new baby growing up thinking their Dad was just a skirt-chaser.'

'You should have thought of that before you hooked up with Lindy Prescott.'

Ella touched her on the arm. 'Let him finish, Mum.'

'What's that?'

'Let him finish. There's more.'

Mum looked back at Dad. 'Well?'

'I started giving Kelman handouts. Not too much to begin with but he seemed satisfied. It probably felt like a lot of money to him. I hated doing it but I figured he'd keep quiet as long as I gave him his meal ticket. And he did. But he wouldn't hand over the photographs and the negatives. Then nine months later he told me Lindy had had a little girl.'

'You fool,' said Mum. 'You stupid fool.'

'I thought he was lying at first. Just making mischief. He told me to check for myself. I rang Lindy. It was the first time we'd spoken since she left the store. She said she'd had a daughter. She was called Imogen. I asked if the girl was mine. She said yes. She could have been lying, I suppose, but I knew she wasn't. She wasn't the type to make things up.'

'So you started giving her money, too.'

'She wouldn't let me. I tried to persuade her, said I'd pay for whatever the baby needed, but she wouldn't take a penny. She said she just wanted me out of her life. By this time Kelman was starting to ask for bigger sums of money, saying he'd go to the newspapers if I didn't pay him and that he'd drag Lindy and her daughter through the mud as well as me and my family if he had to. So I started giving him bigger handouts and that went on for about three years.' Dad's eyes drifted towards the edge of the cliff. 'Until a day ten years ago that I'd give all the money I have to go back and change.'

A squall rippled over them from the sea.

'It was the first of August. The day felt wrong from the moment I woke up. It started calmly enough but by midday a big storm had blown up, just like this one today. It seemed to come out of nothing. I was up here to give Kelman his next handout. We always met at the lighthouse. Twelve noon, first day of every month. I hated having to meet him but he never had a fixed address I could send the money to. God knows, he could have afforded something with the stuff I was giving him, but I think he liked meeting me anyway. It gave him a kick to feel his power over me.'

He stared past them up the slope.

'There was no sign of him so I went into the bracken and climbed up the slope. He was usually late and I'd taken to sketching the lighthouse while I was waiting for him. It calmed me down to do something like that and also gave me an excuse for being here. The wind was getting stronger and stronger and the bracken was brushing against me but I started to draw. I'd only been there a few minutes when I saw a figure down on the coastal path.'

He looked at Ella. 'It was a little girl. She was so like you. I almost thought it was you for a moment. She was even the same sort of age, about three. She had a pretty white dress on and she came running along the coastal path followed by a boy. Great big clumsy kid. He was only about five—you could tell from his face—but he was huge for his age, really huge. Yet for all that he couldn't keep up with her. Kept falling over his own feet. And she was leading him a real dance.'

Fin listened in a daze, trying to make sense of all that had happened, and all that was happening; but he found he could not. He glanced down at Sam, still sleeping in his arms, and pulled him closer, then looked back at Dad. 'What happened?' he said.

'She kept running round him and jumping up at the sky, like someone had thrown a ball over her head and she was trying to catch it. The boy looked really flustered and anxious. He seemed to be trying to get her to stop and come back from the cliff but she broke away suddenly and ran into the bracken. She kept hiding for a bit, then running out, pulling a face at him and disappearing again. It seemed a bit cruel. You could see he adored her and he was obviously upset but she was just making fun of him. She ran into the bracken again and I lost sight of her but she must have crawled up my way because the next thing I knew she came upon me sitting there.'

Dad's face darkened.

'She seemed a bit startled, then when she saw me smiling, she relaxed a bit. I think she was used to people smiling at her. I saw her brother running away down the coastal path. He was shouting to someone but I couldn't see anybody. I know I should have called out to him but I just . . . I don't know . . . I just didn't. I wanted to talk to her. I couldn't believe she looked so much like Ella. Then I understood.'

'Understood what?' said Mum.

'Who she was. I suddenly saw it in her face, even though we'd never met and there was no sign of Lindy anywhere. I just knew it was her.' He took a slow breath. 'I reached out to touch her. I know I shouldn't have. It was stupid. But I just wanted to give her a little pat on the head. Nothing more. She screamed and tried to move back. I should have drawn my hand away—I know that—but I caught her by the arm. I was startled and it was an impulse. I just wanted to reassure her I wasn't going to hurt her. She screamed again. I let go at once and she tore off through the bracken towards the lighthouse. She was out of her mind with panic. She was just running and screaming. I didn't do anything at first—I was too shocked—then I thought of the cliff. I started to run after her, calling to her to stop. That seemed to scare her even more. She burst out of the bracken and headed straight for the edge. I was just a few inches behind her when she . . . she disappeared.'

Another squall flew over them.

'She hit the big rock just below us and slipped into the sea.' He clapped a hand over his face. 'I panicked. I freaked. I didn't know what to do. The boy had disappeared and there was no one else in sight. I picked up my sketchpad and ran. I just ran and ran. I don't know where I went or how long I was out. When I got home, you were all in the garden. It was really stormy by this time but Fin was upset with me because I'd promised to fix the badminton net. So I fixed it and we played badminton. Christ! We played bloody badminton while the body of Imogen Prescott was floating away.'

'I don't believe I'm hearing this,' said Mum. Dad reached out a hand to her but she pushed it angrily away. 'Don't touch me! Don't come near me!'

'Dad,' said Fin, 'you can't know it was Imogen Prescott.'

'It was her.' Dad was crying now. 'It was on the news. That's probably the other place your mum heard Lindy's name.' Mum said nothing. Dad wiped his eyes with the back of his hand. 'It was a big story at the time. The little girl who was playing on the coastal path with her brother and who suddenly disappeared.'

'But why wasn't her mother with her?' said Fin.

'She was, apparently. She was further down the coastal path, just out of sight. The girl had run on ahead to the lighthouse. She wasn't supposed to but she was headstrong.'

'Well, this Lindy woman should have run after her and brought her back.'

'She couldn't. That was the point. The report said she'd sprained an ankle or something and couldn't run. But the boy ran after the girl to try and get her to come back.'

Fin stared down at the sea. 'What happened to the girl's body?' he said.

'It was never found. That's why most people thought she'd been abducted. If she'd fallen over the cliff, you'd have expected the body to be washed up somewhere along the coast and it never was. But the storm got worse as the day went on and during the night it caused the first of the cliff-falls. That pile of boulders to the right of the cave was once part of the rockface and I've been haunted ever since by the thought that her body might be buried underneath.'

'All this,' said Mum, bitterly. 'And you never told me.'

'I was ashamed. I'm still ashamed.'

'And is that it? Or is there more? I hardly dare to ask.'

'There's more. A little.'

'Well, get on with it.'

'Kelman caught up with me the next day. He was just glowing. It made me sick to see him. He apologized in his politest manner for not meeting me at the lighthouse. Then he explained that he'd actually been there all the time. Said he'd spotted Lindy Prescott far down the coastal path and had crept into the bracken near the lighthouse so he could spy on her when she came past. But she never showed. Then he saw the little girl running up the path, followed by her brother, and he stayed put to see what they did.'

Dad shook his head.

'Of all the people to see what happened, it had to be Kelman. Of course, his version had me molesting the girl first and then throwing her over the cliff. I knew he couldn't prove anything and that it was his word against mine but I also knew he could make life intolerable for all of us. So we did a deal.'

'More money.'

'Yes. But this time much more. A big one-off payment.'

'How much?'

'Enough for him to disappear from the area forever and live in some comfort. I knew he'd never get a carrot that big offered to him again. In return he was to give me the photographs and negatives and clear off for good and keep his mouth shut. I didn't expect him to manage the last two but I thought if I could just get the photos and negatives off him, his word would be easy to discredit if he did start mouthing off. Anyway, he accepted.'

'You did all that,' said Mum, her voice still bitter and angry. 'And you said nothing to me.'

'I thought if I just paid the man and got rid of him, we could put it all behind us.'

'We?'

'All right, I could. And Kelman did honour his word up to a point. He gave me the photos and the negatives, and disappeared for ten years. But then he turned up again a few weeks ago, threatening to spill the story if I didn't give him more money. He'd probably already spoken to Ricky Prescott by that time and was just trying it on. I didn't even

190

know Ricky Prescott was in the area or what he looked like. All I remembered was the big bumbling kid on the cliff. And I didn't know Lindy had died either.'

'So what did you say to Kelman?'

'I told him to get lost. Didn't think there was any danger any more. The word of a drunken tramp against mine about things that happened so long ago. I felt fairly confident he didn't have any more photos. If he'd kept any copies, he'd have come straight out and told me so to put pressure on me, but he said nothing. He came back a second time and tried again. That's when Fin saw him. That's the whole story.' He looked at Ella. 'I'm so sorry. I just wish the boy had tried to kill me rather than you. I don't know why he didn't.'

'He wanted you to suffer.' Ella stared at him with contempt. 'It was never about money. He just asked for that so he could spin everything out and make you squirm. He was always going to throw it away. He told me. Before he met Kelman all he remembered of his family was a little sister he loved and was supposed to be looking after when she disappeared, and a mother he loved who died a few months later. He said he felt terrible guilt for leaving Imogen on the cliff and running back to his mum. He thought it was his fault his sister died. When he found out it wasn't, all he wanted was revenge. He said he always intended to kill me.'

Dad shuddered. 'Why didn't he?'

'It was my hair. He said it was just like Imogen's. It upset him so much to see it. He said looking at me felt like looking at the way Imogen would have been if she'd lived. He was even thinking of letting me go after getting Fin to throw away the money. Then he heard Sam.'

'Sam?' said Mum.

'It was over the phone. Ricky was giving instructions to Fin about the money and he heard Sam talking about going to catch the storm. It was exactly what Imogen said to Ricky the day they ran up here.'

'I remember Sam saying that,' said Mum, 'and I remember this Ricky sounding scared. But what did it mean?'

'Ricky had a nightmare when he was a little boy. He told me about it. It was a few days before Imogen went over the cliff. He dreamt there was going to be a terrible storm and it would mean death.'

'Death?'

'Imogen's death. He dreamt this storm was going to come and catch her and take her away forever. He said it had a great foaming mouth and she was being chased into it by some huge, horrible creature. He couldn't see the creature in the dream but he could feel it just behind her, chasing her into the storm. She was screaming and screaming and the creature was only inches behind her, then suddenly she jumped into the foaming mouth—and everything went black. I had the same nightmare when I was in the chamber.'

She looked round at them, her eyes as wild as the wind.

'When the storm blew up on the day Imogen died, Ricky tried to tell her about the nightmare but she just laughed at him. She said the storm wasn't going to catch her. She was going to catch it instead. She was going to jump up into the sky and catch the storm and take it away. When she ran ahead to the lighthouse, Ricky was terrified she was going to die. He ran after her and tried to make her come away but she just made fun of him, jumping up at the sky and shouting "Catch the storm, catch the storm!" and then hiding in the bracken. He ran off in a panic to his mum and by the time they reached the lighthouse, Imogen was gone.'

Ella started to shiver.

'When Ricky heard Sam using Imogen's words, it terrified him. He thought it was a message from her saying he had to go through with his plan and kill me for the sake of revenge. He rowed me to the island and we talked. We talked for ages, about him, about his mum and sister, about Kelman.' She looked at Dad. 'About you. He said I had to die. It was an eye for an eye and a tooth for a tooth. He wanted you to live. He wanted you to feel the same guilt he's felt. He was going to send you an anonymous note telling you where my body was and saying it was your fault that I died. Then he was going to come back ten years from now and kill you, too.'

'Darling,' said Mum, pulling her close, but Ella went on, her voice now faltering.

'We finished talking and . . . and Ricky said it was time. I ran away but he caught me at the top of the island and put a gun to my head. But he didn't pull the trigger. He just held it there. I knew he was trying to make himself do it but he couldn't. He just . . . held it there for ages and ages and I was begging him not to kill me . . . and crying . . . and . . . and then suddenly he took it away and . . . I just went on crying and crying. I was too scared to move. Then I heard him crying, too, and I looked round. He said he was sorry, he couldn't do it, and he went to put the gun in his mouth. I reached out to push it away but it went off by accident into the side of his head. He fell back against the rock. I thought he was dead.'

She burst into tears and Mum held her tight, stroking the back of her head. Dad walked to the edge of the cliff and stared down. 'I'm sorry. I'm sorry.'

'It's too late to be sorry!' Ella screamed at him. 'It's too late!' She narrowed her eyes. 'You should have gone over the cliff, not Imogen.'

Fin felt Sam stir in his arms and looked down to see the boy's eyes opening. Sam stared blearily round at them for a few moments, then he spoke. 'Ella . . . Ella . . . '

Ella broke free from Mum and reached for him. 'Sammy,' she said. Fin passed him over and she pulled him close. 'Sammy,' she murmured, kissing him. 'Sammy.'

Mum put an arm round her. 'Come on,' she said, and they set off with Sam back down the coastal path. Fin made to follow, then froze. The movement by the cliff-edge had been slight but he caught it in the corner of his eye. He spoke at once, knowing he must.

'Dad, don't.'

The movement stopped. He kept his eyes on Mum and Ella and Sam as they made their way down the path, unaware of all this. He wondered where his father's eyes were directed. At him? At them? Or down at the rock that had broken the fall of Imogen Prescott? He spoke again.

'Dad, please don't.' He closed his eyes, unable to look. The sound of the wind felt like a fire raging around him. He waited a few moments, fighting the pictures that rushed into his head, then he steeled himself, opened his eyes and turned. Before him was an empty space.

'No!' he said. He strode to the cliff-edge and stared down in panic at the crashing seas; then he caught another movement in the corner of his eye. He turned towards it and slumped to the ground, the tension draining from him. Away to the left was the figure of his father shuffling down the path after the others. He was bent over like an old man. Walking towards them were Mr and Mrs Meade and two policemen.

19

Ricky Prescott lay in intensive care. He had a drip in his arm, tubes in his mouth, nose, and neck, and leads attached to his chest. A wire ran from a monitor to a clip on one of his fingers. A nurse was bent over the bed, adjusting the bandage on his temple.

Fin watched, still struggling to come to terms with what had happened. The day had passed in a kind of blur. There had been police interviews, journalists turning up at the house, onlookers in the lane and now, in the late afternoon, sitting here with Mum, Dad, Ella, and Sam, he felt spent and confused. The storm had eased only for another to break in his life; and this one, he sensed, would last much longer.

He leaned back in the chair. Everything felt unreal, as though he were an actor playing out a drama and any moment he would walk out of the theatre and back into real life. Yet this was real life and before him was a boy close to losing it. He studied the figure of Ricky Prescott and found he could no longer hate him.

'What chances has he got?' he said to the nurse.

She turned round. 'Hard to say. He's in a bad state. The head wasn't designed to have bullets shot into it.' She looked at Mum. 'Hasn't he got any family?'

'Not any immediate family,' said Mum. 'Well,

there might be a father. The police are trying to trace him.'

'What about the mother?'

'She's dead.' Mum looked round at Dad. He caught her eye and looked away.

'Poor boy,' said the nurse. 'And are there any other relatives?'

'I don't know.'

The nurse glanced back at the figure in the bed. 'Well, let's hope someone's looking out for him.' And she walked over to speak to the consultant by the door.

Fin looked at Ella. She was holding onto Mum's arm as she had done for most of the day. Her eyelids were half-closed. Sam, on the other hand, seemed bright and alert. He was sitting on the floor by himself, his eyes fixed on the bed. Suddenly he spoke.

'Go where?'

'What's that, sweetheart?' said Mum.

He didn't look up at her. His eyes were on the figure of Ricky Prescott.

'Go where?' he said again.

The figure didn't move, save for the rise and fall of the chest. Mum bent down and stroked Sam's head but still he didn't look at her. He hadn't even heard her. All he heard was the voice speaking inside his head.

It was a funny voice, not like the little girl's voice at all. That was beautiful. He loved that voice. He missed it. He knew he wouldn't hear it again. He didn't know why. He just knew she was gone. But this other voice was different. Not nasty, not scary. Just different.

Let me go, it said.

'Go where?'

Just go.

'Are you going to die?'

'Sam?' said Mum. But Sam heard only the voice.

You're holding me back.

'I'm not.'

You are.

Sam started to cry. He hadn't meant to cry. He was trying to be brave like everybody else but he couldn't stop himself. The voice spoke again.

I'm sorry.

'What for?'

I'm sorry.

'Sam?' said Mum again.

He heard her this time. He looked round and saw her face close to his, and Fin's and Ella's and Dad's, too, all watching intently. Fin knelt down beside him.

'Sammy? Who are you talking to?'

Sam looked back at the figure in the bed.

'I don't want you to die,' he said.

But this time he heard no answer.

Fin stood by the kitchen window, staring out. Dusk had fallen and the garden was slipping from view under a shroud of grey. He felt Mum's hand on his shoulder.

'I've disconnected the phones,' she said. 'I'll go mad if another journalist rings up. Or turns up.' She looked out of the window. 'Can you see anybody in the lane?'

'I think they've all gone.'

'No doubt they'll be back.' Mum drew the curtains across.

'El's still in her room,' he said. 'I knocked but she didn't answer.'

'You'll have to be patient, Fin.' Mum looked at him. 'You'll have to give her time.' She pulled him to her. 'Just be there for her, OK? For as long as it takes. That's the best thing you can do for her.'

'OK.' He held onto her.

'I'm so proud of you,' she said.

'I'm proud of you, too. You're not bad for a mum.'

'Praise indeed.'

'I've checked Sammy. He's still sleeping.'

She gave a chuckle. 'And how many times is that?'

'What?'

'How many times is that you've been round to check everyone's OK?'

'I don't know. I just—'

'It's all right.' She gave him a squeeze. 'I'm not making fun of you. Quite the opposite.'

They fell silent, still holding each other, and he listened for sounds up in Ella's room. There were none. He thought of how frightened and vulnerable she'd seemed on the island; how frightened and vulnerable she still seemed. How frightened and vulnerable he himself now felt.

'Mum?'

'Yes, darling?'

'Are you and Dad going to split up?'

'I don't know.' She gave a sigh. 'I just don't know.'

'Where is he?'

199

'He said he was going down to the boat to tidy things up.'

'He's been gone ages.'

'Yes.' Her voice was flat, listless. He remembered that moment by the cliff-edge, that moment Mum knew nothing about, and pushed the image from his mind.

'Mum?'

'Um?'

'Before the police spoke to me, Dad took me on one side. He said he'd told them everything and I was to do the same. I wasn't to miss anything out.'

'I know. He said the same thing to Ella and me.'

'But what for?'

'I suppose he wants to clear the air. Get the whole thing out in the open. Sort of a confession.'

'So the police know everything?'

'Yes.'

He thought of Lindy Prescott and her little girl. Dad's little girl, the little girl who looked like Ella; and died.

'Is Dad going to get into trouble with the law?'

'I doubt it.' Mum gave another sigh. 'He's in a mess and the papers'll have a field day but he hasn't actually committed a crime. The only person who could accuse him of anything is Kelman and he'll have enough on his plate when the police start questioning him about blackmail.'

'But there's no proof of that either.'

'I know. Neither of them can prove anything against the other so I don't imagine anyone'll be charged. Unless Kelman admits to the blackmail and that's hardly likely.'

She started to pull away but he held on to her. She stopped at once and drew him close again.

'What is it, darling?'

'I'm worried about Ella. She could get charged with shooting Ricky.'

'No, she won't.' Mum stroked the back of his head. 'I'm sure it'll be all right. She's told the police what happened. Ricky obviously can't tell his side of things but I'll be very surprised if it doesn't get put down as attempted suicide.'

He thought of the figure in the hospital bed; and Ella upstairs, silent, unreachable.

'Mum?'

'Yes, my love.'

'What's going to happen now? What's Dad going to do?'

'I don't know. Resign as a magistrate, throw himself into his work, keep his head down and wait for all this to pass—I can't say what's going to happen. But that's not what this is all about.'

She pulled back and looked him in the face.

'It's not about what happens, Fin. What Dad does or what the world does.' She searched his eyes. 'It's about trust. Don't you see? I trusted him. Ella trusted him. We all trusted him. And now that trust is gone.' She frowned. 'And I don't know how we'll ever get it back.'

Ella woke in the night, the terror still with her. She opened her mouth to call out, then sank back with relief. She was not in the cave. She was in her room.

The storm that had raged in the dream was gone. She was safe and sound in her bed, and the ancient house was still. She sat up suddenly.

No, there was something—a noise, a real noise, downstairs. She listened for it again but silence had fallen once more. She thought of Fin. He'd go down and check it out. She slipped out of bed and made her way to the landing. Fin's door was ajar and she peeped round it. He was fast asleep.

She listened again. There were no further sounds but the house felt creepy. She walked towards the head of the stairs. Sam's door was open and he, too, was sleeping. He looked so beautiful lying there. She wanted to pick him up and hold him.

Tap!

She jumped. It was a metallic sound, just as before, and again coming from the sitting room. She shivered as the memories flooded back. She looked round at Fin's room, at Mum and Dad's room, then clenched her fists and turned back to the stairs. She'd faced this before. She had to face it again. She took a deep breath and started to make her way down towards the hall.

Tap!

She kept on walking, softly, slowly. At the foot of the stairs she stopped and gazed towards the sitting room. The door was half-open and she stared through the gap. There was no light on in the room but she could see that the curtains were drawn back. She crept as far as the door and stopped again, listening for sounds inside the room.

Nothing. Only a deep, ominous silence.

Tap!

She gave a start, yearning to scream, to run back upstairs, but she knew she could not. Whatever this was, she had to confront it, just as she'd done before. She took another deep breath and peered round the door.

Dad was standing by the window, his back to her. Behind him was an open suitcase with some clothes roughly thrown into it. He didn't turn, didn't seem to know she was there. He was leaning forward, his brow against the window pane, one arm over his head, pressed against the glass. The hand moved back, then stabbed forward.

Tap!

She watched. He was holding something and tapping it against the glass. It looked like a key—yes, it was a key, one of the car keys. She could see it now. He tapped it once more, then turned and slumped to the floor, his back against the radiator; and then he saw her.

He said nothing. He did not move. She walked forward and stood over him. He was weeping, silently, his eyes staring up at her, then suddenly, as though her presence unlocked something inside him, he opened his mouth and started to throw out great wrenching sobs, so violent that they frightened her and made her step back. He did not touch her. He simply cried, his eyes never leaving her as the tears rolled from them.

She watched, unable to hold him, unable to move away, and gradually he calmed down. They looked at each other in silence. She felt her own tears moving now and turned towards the door. He did not speak. She hurried through to the hall and up the first of the stairs, then stopped, breathing hard; and turned, and walked back. He was still slumped against the radiator, his eyes moist with pain.

'Don't go,' she said.

20

To Fin the summer seemed to pass like a series of slow-motion images so vivid he felt they would haunt him forever. Yet when autumn came with its mists and rain and swirling leaves, he found to his surprise that only one picture remained.

The Pengrig lighthouse.

He didn't know why. He hadn't even been back there—none of them had—yet it hovered over his thoughts and dreams like a spectre of all that had happened, all that he felt. But at least life could go on again. The media interest had died down; no one was going to be charged with any crime; and Dad was still with them.

Yet things were different. Billy and Angie didn't come over so much now and Mr Aldridge had stopped walking his dog up the lane. Fin didn't care; he was just glad to have the family together again. But they, too, had changed. Mum and Dad were awkward with each other and Ella was wary of everyone, even him. Only Sam seemed the same. Despite the shock on the cliff and all that followed, he'd simply carried on with his life and his play as though nothing had happened.

The half-term holidays broke with dark clouds sweeping in from the south-west. Mum called up the stairs. 'Fin! Come on! We're waiting!'

He found her in the lane, standing by the car. Ella was already sitting on the backseat with Sam, reading him a story. He was snuggled under her arm, his eyes wide open as he gazed, listening, at the book. Mum was staring towards the garden and Fin could guess what she was looking at.

Sure enough the figure was there, over by the stable. Dad had changed so much. He seemed to have aged ten years and hardly went in to work any more. He'd delegated most of the running of the business to others and the energy he'd once put into his career now went into the garden. He seemed scarcely to leave it these days. During the summer he'd attacked the weeds so fiercely Fin doubted there could be any left; and now that autumn was here, he'd started planting: flowers and shrubs, to begin with, and now trees. He'd raised the wall on the far side of the paddock to create a windbreak, building it himself brick by brick, and now, under its protection, he had laburnum, maple, bird cherry, acacia, and mountain ash, and all kinds of species Fin had never heard of. He watched as his father carried yet another sapling into the enclosure.

'Mum?' he said.

'Yes, darling?'

'When's Dad going to come back to us?'

'When he's ready. When we're ready.' She paused. 'Not for a while yet.'

Fin looked round at her and saw her smiling back at him.

'Come on,' she said.

They climbed into the car. Mum started the engine and they drove off down the lane. 'Let's hope the rain keeps off,' she said.

'The forecast's not good,' said Fin.

It was certainly dark overhead. He looked round and tried to catch Sam's eye but the little boy seemed interested only in the pictures in the book and the story unrolling in the soft music of Ella's voice. They arrived at Peneventon Lodge to find Ricky out of bed and in his wheelchair, a nurse bending over him to wipe the saliva from his mouth. She looked round as they approached.

'Morning, Shirley,' said Mum.

'Morning.' The nurse smiled at them, then bent down to Sam. 'Good morning, Sam.'

'Good morning, Mrs Nurse.'

She laughed and straightened up. 'That was good timing. Ricky's just finished breakfast.'

'How is he?' said Mum.

'He's OK. I just wish he had some more people coming to see him. If it weren't for all of you, I don't know what we'd do. Still—' She glanced at Sam. 'At least he's got his favourite visitor here. He was distraught the other day when you didn't bring Sam along.'

Sam had taken Ricky's hand and was playing with the fingers. Ricky looked down at him. 'Gah!' he said.

'Hi, Ricky,' said Sam.

Fin watched. It was so strange, this friendship. Ricky's head was rolling from side to side as it did most of the time but his eyes never wavered from Sam's face. Mum lowered her voice and spoke to the nurse.

'It's weird. I think he sees Ricky as a kind of big new Teddy. And have you noticed these little conversations they keep having? With Sam doing all the talking?'

'Yes.' The nurse watched Sam for a moment. 'I'm not quite sure how much Ricky understands. We try and communicate with him here as best we can but it's difficult with patients as brain-damaged as he is to know just how much is getting through. And obviously he can't talk back.'

'Well, Sam seems to have an ongoing dialogue with him. But maybe he's making it up.'

'Maybe.' The nurse frowned. 'But I'll tell you one thing I do know for certain. Ricky's eyes light up every time that little boy comes near him. They don't do that for anyone else.' She looked round at Ella. 'And how are you?'

'Fine. I'm . . . I'm fine.'

The nurse looked at her hard for a moment, then smiled. 'Good,' she said.

'Can we take Ricky out in the garden?' said Fin.

'Why not? But keep to the path, can you? The grass is still a bit wet after all this rain we've been having.' She glanced out of the window. 'And it looks like we might be in for a bit more. I'll just pop Ricky's jacket on him.' She fetched the jacket and deftly slipped it on him. 'Right, then. Shoes.'

'I can do the shoes,' said Sam.

'All right, Sam. Thank you very much.' She handed him the shoes. 'There you go.'

Fin caught Mum's eye and saw her smile. Sam loved putting Ricky's shoes on for him but it always took him ages. Fin bent down to help.

'I'll do it myself,' said Sam.

'OK, Sammy.'

He left Sam to struggle with the shoes and looked into Ricky's eyes. They were a smoky blue and nothing like the ones he had pictured in the days when he had demonized the face. He wondered what they saw when they looked at him. He hoped it wasn't an enemy.

The shoes were on at last and Sam was doing up the laces. He wasn't very good at this and Ella or Mum usually had to distract him at some point so that Fin could retie them while he wasn't looking. Sam stopped suddenly and looked up at Ricky.

'Which one?'

Ricky made a mumbling noise.

'What's he saying, Sam?' said Fin.

'The left shoe's not done up prop'ly.'

Sam untied it and tried again, then looked up at Ricky for approval. Ricky wagged his head and Sam grinned. Clearly the shoe was now OK.

'Let's go,' said Mum.

'Can you manage on your own?' said the nurse.

'No problem,' said Fin.

He took the wheelchair and pushed Ricky out into the garden. The sky was almost black now and the wind was growing stronger. Sam ran alongside, still playing with Ricky's hand, then suddenly he let go and looked round.

'Ricky wants to know when you're going back to the lighthouse.'

Fin gave a start. Sam's eyes were fixed on Ella, then they turned and looked straight at him. He glanced at Ella. 'Do you want to go?'

She was silent for a moment, her lips pursed tightly together, then she turned to Mum. 'Is it OK?'

'Of course it's OK,' said Mum. 'You don't need my permission to go for a walk.'

Sam winked at Ricky. 'I promise,' he said.

'What's he saying, Sam?' said Mum.

'He's telling me to be careful if I go to the lighthouse.'

'He's right. No going near the cliff-edge again. Promise?'

'I just promised Ricky.'

'Well, I want you to promise me, too.'

'I promise.'

But they didn't go to the lighthouse that day. By noon it was raining hard and squalls were driving in from the sea. Sam didn't seem bothered and went up to his room to play but Fin felt uneasy. He knew it wasn't just the tension he always felt after seeing Ricky—it was something else; and Ella's face told him she felt it, too.

But there was no stirring from the house. The wind and rain increased as the afternoon wore on and by night-time a full storm was raging, the first since that day back in the summer. When he woke the next morning, the wind was as strong as ever but the rain had stopped. He looked at Ella over the breakfast table.

'Do you still want to come?' he said.

Her eyes answered no, but she nodded.

'Well, make sure you wrap up,' said Mum. 'It's very blustery out there and I think there's more rain on the way. I can't see your father getting much done in the garden today.' She glanced out of the window at him, then turned and looked at Sam, who was carefully negotiating his way through a boiled egg. 'Do you still want to go with them to the lighthouse?'

'I'm playing with my friends today.'

'Which friends are those, Sam?'

'It's a secret.'

'OK.'

Sam went on eating for a moment, his attention all on the egg, then suddenly he looked up. His eyes moved slowly from face to face. 'What are you all laughing at me for?' he said.

'We're not laughing at you, sweetheart,' said Mum. 'We're just smiling.'

'What for?'

'Never mind.' She kissed him. 'Finish your breakfast.' And Sam turned back to his egg.

Fin and Ella set off at a brisk pace. The ground was wet and the wind buffeted them the moment they left the house. Dad was over in the rockery, bent low to the ground, but he saw them and waved, then returned to his work. They strode off down the lane and soon reached the forked path. Fin stopped and caught Ella by the arm.

'Wait,' he said.

'What's wrong?'

'We're rushing.'

'What?'

'We're rushing. We're tearing along. We're almost running.'

She looked down. 'I just . . . I suppose . . . '

'It's OK.' He stroked her arm. 'I know. You want to get it over with.'

She nodded and he smiled at her.

'I do, too,' he said. 'But let's go easy.'

They walked on, slowly now, but he sensed the tension still in her, and in himself. The sea opened before them, grey and restless with whitecaps cresting the surface. They reached the signpost by the coastal path and set off in the direction of the Pengrig lighthouse.

But the Pengrig lighthouse was no longer there.

They stopped and stared in silence. Where the old light had been, there was now only an empty space. They walked on, neither speaking, and as they drew near, they saw what had happened. The cliff had collapsed during the storm and the lighthouse had plunged with it. They stopped at a safe distance and surveyed the devastation. Everything had gone: the building, the fence, whole chunks of the cliff. A mountain of broken rock now rose from the sea, blocking what had once been the entrance to the cave.

'It's over,' said Fin.

Ella didn't answer. He turned to look at her and saw she was crying.

'It's over for Imogen Prescott,' she said.

There was a silence between them, broken only by the mewing of the gulls and the pounding of the surf. Then he understood. He looked down, ashamed.

'I'm sorry,' he said.

She kissed him on the cheek and started back the way they had come. He watched her for a moment, then turned and ran his eye over the fallen cliff and the islands offshore. Far out to sea a wave was forming, a green wall of rolling power that curled up like a tongue licking the sky. It rippled towards him, rising, rising, then broke with a crash against the base of the cliff. He stared down at the foaming sea. Mum was right. He had to be patient, had to give Ella time, had to just be there for her; and so he would, for as long as it took. He looked up and saw more waves rolling in, but he didn't wait to see them break. Instead he turned and ran after Ella, and caught her up, and they set off together back towards Polvellan.